THE THIRD TALE OF LA CROIX DE BOIS

NATURE ABHORS A VACUUM

Andy Stonard

Copyright © 2023 Andy Stonard
All rights reserved.

Andy loves to write. He also loves listening to everyone's stories and tales and always has done. He lives in France with his wife Teresa.

In the past, he has worked in alcohol and drug treatment services and also in policy both in the UK and internationally. In that time he would regularly speak at conferences and meetings. Then in France as a gardener. In between this he tries to write.

He has written two books - 'A glass half full', on alcohol use and misuse and 'In search of the ancients' on his travels around England and Wales with a group of mates looking at neolithic sites and pondering what they were all about whilst enjoying the banter that only a group of men can conjure up.

The 'La Croix de Bois' series is his first foray into fiction.

La Croix de Bois

The village of La Croix de Bois is without doubt lovely. Tourists who visit it refer to it as beautiful, soulful, pretty and idyllic. Some have been heard to refer to it as like living in paradise.

Many of the villagers would agree with that sentiment. It can be paradise to live in but work hard to keep it like that.

On the Eagles album is a track called the Last Resort. The song finishes with:

*You call some place paradise
Kiss it goodbye.*

In the bible, the garden of Eden was a paradise but it had a snake lurking in it.

Chapter 1 - The weather

I am aware that most of the stories that I have told you around La Croix de Bois have happened when the weather has been sunny and warm.

Well today, it is raining.

Although raining does not really describe it.

'To say that it is bucketing down would also be an understatement,' Jean Paul, my friend says to me as we shelter under the awning by the Mayor's building. I can only describe it as monsoonal.

The door opens behind us, as our good friend Gerard walks out.

'It's like a monsoon,' he shouted, agreeing with me over the noise of the rainfall. In the village square the water was bubbling out of the drains as the sheer amount of water overwhelmed the entire drainage system.

'This is the second time this week this has happened. They told us that last Tuesday there was the equivalent of a month's rainfall in just seven hours' Jean Paul said.

'And this one seems as bad' Gerard said

'Worse I'd say' Jean Paul added.

Like everywhere else in the world, we were noticing how much the weather patterns seemed to be changing. In May and June it had not rained once, which was also something new. For the last three years, frosts had become an unusual occurrence, whereas before then January and February mornings were usually white and crisp.

Then this year we had a week of between minus 8 and minus 14, which again was unheard of over the last seven years.

The awning was proving to be inadequate in such a downfall and we headed back into the building.

It was there that we heard the secretary talking on the telephone to the engineer who manages the river and tributaries locally saying that the river had burst its banks just below the village.

Predictably, Jean Paul announced that we were looking at global warming.

'Hope you guys don't have a beach side apartment in the

Maldives' he said to the two of us, 'because it's gonna be disappearing pretty soon as the sea levels rise.

We both laughed.

'Listen, after the last ice age the sea levels rose by over 200 metres as the ice melted. Two hundred metres!!! Before that you could have walked to England overland. Well that's not strictly true as there was a bloody great river running between what is now England and France.'

'So you would need to have a boat? Who would want to do that?' Gerard asked.

'I'm just saying that is what you could do. Jersey was some hills across the plateau of the bay that St Mont Michel sits in. Then the sea rushed in. That was global warming on speed.'

'And this is now' Gerard announced looking out of the door into the square, which now looked like a low level pond, 'you are probably correct Jean Paul, the question is what is anyone doing about it apart from talking and worrying?'

Any answer from Jean Paul was interrupted by a tremendous bolt of lighting and then a long rumbling and rolling thunder that made the glass in the window vibrate and sent us into silence.

Chapter 2 - The past and the present

La Croix de Bois is an attractive village nestled in a valley which has a river running through it. It is a village of contrasts. On the one hand it can be described as a sleepy and safe place but like everywhere else it has its moments of excitement, and it has its festivals and in the summer, it has its tourists.

It is my idea of paradise on earth and my view, I know, is shared by many people here, so much so that it is protected as best as it can be by those who feel this way. That protection comes in a multitude of levels as my tales will tell.

In addition to what these individuals do, there is almost a feeling that something greater also cares about this lovely little village. It is difficult to explain. There is nothing tangible to prove nor demonstrate this. It is just a sense, a feeling that some of us have. It is not something that has just happened recently. Talking with some of the older villagers you get the sense that it is something that has built up over time, something that has evolved possibly over centuries.

Is that possible?

In France and especially in Brittany the myths and fables are strong and even in the twenty-first century with its modern technology and global influences for good and bad, these myths and fables still survive and are handed down. They have survived the very best that religion could throw at it, along with despot rulers and countless invaders. So why should it cease now?'

There has always been a thin veil between the past and the present and the living and the dead. The same thin veil between this world and other worlds that you cannot see. The myths tell us that on special days or times this veil can be seen through such times as All Souls Night and Christmas Eve.

Similarly, there is a belief, that some Breton born share with the Welsh, that a heavy mist or fog can enable you to travel through this veil across time.

I cannot say any of this with any certainty apart from I know and see what I see.

There are others who understand these phenomena and have special abilities and insights, who live and share my life in the village of La Croix de Bois. I have come to understand that for some they knowingly use these abilities but for others they are beautifully oblivious to their talent and go about using these abilities in perfect ignorance or as a learned behaviour that seem normal, like driving a car or cooking.

I have been amazed at some of what has happened in La Croix de Bois and how terrible crimes can be committed and turned into positive outcomes for the better good. I have witnessed a murder, have lost a close friend in another murder, discovered hidden treasure that came from bad sources, uncovered wonderful items from history and heard stories and deeds that have made me weep with joy.

I have seen different sides to people that I never thought existed and I have met people who many would consider bad or dangerous people in their pasts, but whose actions in the present could be seen as good deeds.

I have always tried not to be judgemental but have often failed in my past, but I have learned not to judge anyone anymore. I now realise that we are often driven by powers and influences beyond our control. Of course there are always choices that we all have but sometimes those choices are all unpalatable.

We can always make excuses and some of us make those

excuses all of our lives. Sometimes it feels easier to make those excuses to do nothing or turn away, when the right thing to do is to act. We are all capable of making things better and just as skilled at making things worse or doing nothing.

The Chinese would call it the ying and yang. My own interpretation is that mother nature at all levels abhors a vacuum. Winds are created where there is a difference in pressure and the air is simply moved from a place of high pressure to fill in for a low pressure.

I guess my interpretation of this balance is difficult to grasp, until you recognise this balancing act is a constant and always happening. There is no settled state, apart from death and even then our atoms are starting to transfer themselves somewhere else.

With the wind there may be a delightful couple of days of what we see as sunny settled weather but, elsewhere things are afoot to move this high pressure away to fill in for a low somewhere else.

I am probably contradicting myself, saying that La Croix de Bois seems special and then saying that there is no settled state in this world. I am old and sometimes...no, often foolish, as I am often told.

I must apologise. I have too much time on my hands today and I am rambling. The main tale I want to tell you this time has in some ways been ongoing for a long time, even centuries but it is a tale that I can tell because I think that it has reached a conclusion and now must be told. Naturally of course it is also intermingled with numerous others.

Chapter 3 – After the first few waves of Covid

Surprisingly, no one in La Croix de Bois became infected with the first two rounds of covid 19. No one knew why that was the case. It just worked out that way.

The doctors in the village talked about it because they would have noticed and of course the beautiful pharmacist noticed but no one else really talked about it because half of the people never noticed and the other half were not surprised.

Things like that never happened in La Croix de Bois. Like the rest of France, plenty of people had ailments or aches and pains - it was part and parcel of growing old but so was flu and covid and other ghastly illnesses, but most people in the village rarely seemed to suffer with the flu. Common colds and coughs of course. Why was this another fact of life in La Croix de Bois? No one knew.

The plans for the mini hydro powered turbine that would replace the old wheel were complete. One third of the houses in La Croix de Bois were now fitted with solar panels and the geothermal or underground heating system had been installed across all the outlying farms and their barns.

The plan was for La Croix de Bois to be able to export electricity to the French national grid rather than importing it. The aspiration was that everyone in the village would eventually not be paying for their electricity.

Like covid, no-one outside, apart from EDF who were the national electricity suppliers knew this fact and no-one in La Croix de Bois advertised that fact. No-one wanted unwelcome news hounds around the village and people setting them up as an example of an eco village but more importantly and pertinent was where the money had come from to start this all up.

The proceeds of the drug money had paid for this. The money came from men and women who had become addicted to the drugs that dealers sold and all the misery that came from it. To pay for these drugs the addicts had jewelry and money to pay for their drugs or engage in nefarious acts to earn it.

The money and jewelry had then been stolen by a criminal gang from a drug gang.

This transfer of funds based on crime and people's misery had a direct connection to the village of La Croix de Bois. That is where the misery ended and instead, it became a force for being positive.

To make that connection, one of the gang had seen fit to hide the money and jewelry by burying it in the ground by the village's old hill fort and ancient caves that tumbled down to the river. The magnificent Menhir that had stood above the village for 4,000 years watched impervious as the money and then the jewelry was crudely buried by an anxious gang member.

When we discovered it quite by accident, we were uncertain what to do at first but between us, and the powerful influences we never realised that we were under had us putting it all to good measure. We never kept it. Well, not really, at least not ourselves directly but I guess we knew that what we would do would benefit us indirectly and if it did not achieve that, then it made us feel bloody good about ourselves.

But of course, everything has consequences and as I have said, 'nature abhors a vacuum', so when we watched the consequences of what we had done on national TV in the village bar, we celebrated and it was a round of drinks for everyone. In fact it was two rounds - one from the Mayor and one from Marcel and Maria, the bar owners.

What we could never have appreciated at the time was

what our actions would unleash

Sometimes the collective conscious makes great decisions that one person can never make and when this happens it is all the more powerful. The story filled the newspapers and TV for days. The social media was alive with speculation and theories but the secret was safe with the good citizens.

What was particularly gratifying with the jewelry was that within this horde were two Legion d'Honneur medals - one of them was for a soldier from the North African Campaign in the Second World War, both of which were repatriated to their original owners and their families.

That collective conscience had created a defining moment in the lounge of my friend Gerard's home. In attendance was the Mayor, Madame Lebouf and Cristal Lamarr, the pharmacist, who is also one of the Commune Councillors (*conseillers municipaux*). Jean Paul, Gerard and myself.

The Mayor had included Madame Lebouf, who knew everyone in the village, its history and was the essence of discretion and always had been. The beautiful pharmacist who was also a brilliant administrator was part of this small group. Her name is Cristal Lamarr - not only a pharmacist and a councillor on the commune but she was a healer. A magikal healer, with the perfect job for a healer.

From that meeting, Jean Paul also got his wish - the last of the money was being put into the empty Hotel and Restaurant to create a communally run restaurant. The owner had abandoned it three years ago and put it up for sale. He had simply grown too fat and idle to run it anymore and frankly no one in the village apart from the unwary tourist could stomach any of the food, so once the tourist season had finished the restaurant was devoid of victims.

Jean Paul and the mayor had persuaded a couple of friends, Joseph and Stefan, to manage the Hotel and Restaurant. They had met years ago at catering college and both worked in busy restaurants in Paris and then individually decided to take their talents back to Brittany where they were determined to create and develop something different and this was their opportunity.

Jean Paul had been dubious to start with as both had a background in Pizza. Jean Paul was ready to terminate the interview there and then because of his near hatred of the Pizza. It was even something that had killed his friend Roger.

But Joseph and Stefan had calmly explained that Pizzas

were low cost, high price and turnover. Rents were not cheap and salaries for staff even higher with the social charges. With a rent free building and low overheads, then yes they would still make Pizzas but also they would cook what they had learned to cook and would experiment and would run Jean Paul's communal dream.

They blitzed the old place, then they bought in women and men who could cook but who had never worked commercially, on a guest basis.

The timetable was running perfectly.

Naturally, there were the classic French dishes but there were themed weekends just as he had envisaged, Indian and Thai nights, Tapas nights, even a Greek night that included plate smashing. In a village that was rural like La Croix de Bois, the chance of eating famous dishes from around the World was pretty slim unless you tried to cook them yourself.

One of the men was Randy, who everyone who had ever been invited to his home for dinner expressed the fact that they had been in culinary heaven. So naturally Scottish Randy was serving up a storm once a month, not only with his homemade oatcakes, cheddar cheese and homemade chilli jam, which was spicy to say the least, but his Oxtail soup, Scottish salmon, along with clootie dumplings became a great hit. He had fifty eight guests in for Burns night on a cold January night for haggis, neeps and tatties, a whisky sauce and poetry read by diners from the dirty bard himself.

The Sunday carvery was also a welcome addition to the menu and always attracted a good attendance.

There was even an American Independence Day with Jambalaya and Ribs and Fries, Sweet Potato Pie, that the American contingent from the area cooked.

Others who had settled from other lands produced Paella and Schnitzels, Persian lamb and apricot stew and Hungarian Goulash. Not to be outdone a number of British ladies started to produce meat pies, Cornish pasties and sausage rolls for lunchtime.

On Tuesday lunchtime it was a free dinner for the pensioners of the village and the restaurant was getting more and more booked out for birthday and family parties and even wedding receptions.

The faces of satisfaction on those who came in and cooked and their friends who came and ate was wonderful. I have rarely seen Jean Paul so happy. And there was Joseph and Stefan working diligently and attentively behind them all. Jean Paul referred to them as mincing behind the amateur chefs, everywhere but attentive or mincing they did a brilliant job. All quite illegal of course as none of these 'chefs' had food and hygiene qualifications within the employment laws of France, which is why Joseph or Stefan took it in turns to be there.

Chapter 4 - Guys' Cliff

Guys' Cliff is a mysterious abandoned Manoir on the cliffs overlooking the river about three kilometres outside of La Croix de Bois.

The building was first started in the 18th century and completed over fifty years. Ever since it was built, it has always had a troubled history.

Clearly there was another building before the Manoir was constructed. Some people believe that it was the original site of a Hospitaliers building that was torn down and left as rubble over the centuries until an enterprising business man from Paris decided to develop it.

The Hospitaliers are a movement that developed and worked hand in hand with the Red Monks or Knight Templars as they are more famously known. In simple terms, the Hospitaliers were the medical and health teams. Founded to tend to wounded knights in the crusades in the middle east, they had evolved into running sanctuaries for the sick and ill in France and across other parts of Europe.

The positioning of Guys' Cliff would make sense with this

scenario as it was close to the crossroads between the coast and the fairs and markets at Pleboulle, the tower at Montbran with Rennes, all of which were controlled by the Templars far to the south. It was also only a few kilometres from Vilde Guingalan, which the Knight Templars had founded and built, to the east and onwards to Dinan. To the west lay St Brieuc and onwards to Guingamp.

Guys' cliff is viewed as a Manoir. Its roof was still intact and reasonably good condition. There were a couple of windows that were boarded up but inside the huge beams still held the structure together and the internal stone staircase took it up over three storeys.

It was a magnificent structure set in 81 hectares (200 acres) of ground that swept down to the river.

But its history is troubled. Very troubled indeed. I found it fascinating that it sits at a distance from La Croix de Bois. Local people speak of the difference between La Croix de Bois and Guys' Cliff. People in the area state that the village of La Croix de Bois opens up your heart, while Guys' Cliff closes it. La Croix de Bois is light and airy, while Guys' Cliff is dark and moody. Many people will say that they have an uncomfortable feeling being near Guys' Cliff and its claustrophobic atmosphere. The whole place has a foreboding and sometimes an intimidating presence even in the sunlight.

Why this is, I learned one day talking with a man that the pharmacist, Cristal Lamarr introduced me to years ago. His name is Albert Jules. Some people refer to him as wise Albert or old Albert. However, most people know him as the Professor. He is actually a retired professor from Rennes. Albert was born in the La Croix de Bois and grew up there until the world of academia took him away. That same life of academia and research has taken him all over the globe but in the last twenty years he has been back at home in **La Croix de Bois**.

He sat with me and explained the troubled history of Guys' Cliff from its origins to its various owners through the ages and the stories of demonic worship and black magic to bankruptcy and decay. Strangely, he explained, 'very little had been recorded or written down over centuries and perhaps the stories handed down by word and mouth had taken on a life of their own'.

'However', he continued 'unmarked graves had been uncovered there in the 1700s and in 1852 there was the famous story of a man who had farmed close to Guy's Cliff and one night he had fled into La Croix de Bois, screaming hysterically that he had seen the devil in the grounds with a following of worshipers. The then Mayor took him into his own home where the man shivered and shook for a number of hours and then passed out. In the morning he was dead.'

Albert Jules, the Professor said 'like anything that has history but has been abandoned, it has attracted intrigue and interest. As children, local people will recall being told to never go there by their parents and grandparents, but of course they did. Already excited but in fear many of them had run home terrified at what they thought that they had seen or heard.'

'Inevitably, these fears and thoughts stayed in the memory and were accepted as childhood experiences and scary stories from adults. It never occurred to them that their fear may have been rooted by an actual demonic power rather than silly stories and childhood imagination.'

Of course, he continued, as a child any building or place was more scary in your imagination. The woods always were a darker and sinister place.'

'Now we sit and watch horror films and cover our eyes and hide behind the sofa. Then you remember your childhood experiences and the memory has them embedded in such a way that could not really be true and laugh at those memories.'

'People will tell you that until you travel up Guys' Cliff as an adult, then you are shocked that those memories were actually very real. Even worse is that in some ways it is even more terrifying what you see in front of you as an adult. I believe that there is something fundamentally wrong with Guys Cliff,' the Professor concluded.

I knew that Jean Paul and Gerard had gone there, and had not gone back and were in no hurry to go back.

This in many ways spoke volumes.

Chapter 5 - Farid Khalil the Beekeeper

Farid Khalil lived in Daraa in southern Syria. He was a beekeeper. He kept 150 hives. The bees were honey bees and native to southern Syria. He had followed in the footsteps of beekeepers over thousands of years. Syria was considered to be the region that saw the birthplace of farming. It was the dream place for those interested in beekeeping.

Farid's hives are simple wooden boxes that he places horizontally next to one another and then stacks them in piles. He has kept two old traditional hives, one made from terracotta and one made from the trunk of a cork tree, as keepsakes from times gone by.

Syria belongs to one of those countries lucky enough to have a native species of honey bees. The name of the honey bee is *'apis mellifera syriaca'* and they are found everywhere in the country as well as in Jordan, Lebanon and the northern part of Iraq. In this region they have remained genetically pure. In addition, they are very well adapted to their habitat and are very resistant to droughts.

In 2010 across parts of the middle east, what came to be known as the Arab Spring began, mainly in Egypt but it had the effect of stirring up the demand for change.

A year later, there were rumblings of discontent within Syria. On 6th March 2011, in the city of Daraa, between 12 and 15 teenagers were arrested for daubing anti-regime graffiti, in what was seen as copying other groups from that Arab Spring.

The arrest was followed by rumours of torture and beatings of those arrested. This in turn led to more demonstrations to have them released and to learn the truth of what was going on. These demonstrations quickly escalated into armed conflict.

By 31st March, Daraa had been occupied by large numbers of the security forces, who were responsible for killing at least 31 demonstrators outside the Omari Mosque.

At the end of April and early May, the Syrian army under control of President Bashar al Assad's brother, moved in cutting water and electricity and they started shooting at any dissent on the streets and arresting anyone they thought was involved. President Assad's father had put down the rebellion with brutal effect and now his son was doing the same.

By the middle of May, the army withdrew. There was condemnation both within Syria and Internationally but it fell on deaf ears. The numbers of dead ranged from 240 to over a 1,000, depending on who was making the claims, and the wounded ran into many more. Some of those who had been killed had been left on the streets and some were later discovered in unmarked graves.

It was the start of the Syrian War and quickly spread to all corners of Syria from the Kurdish north to various factions across the country. Some parts of the army remained loyal to Assad and others did not. It was also the start of ISIS as a power in the country.

Farid Khalil the beekeeper lived just west of the town of Daraa with 150 bee hives of his own. He also helped others with their beekeeping. It was long hours and hot work but the honey produced earned him a reasonable living. He was married to Fatima and they had three children, Jemal, their son and two daughters Yara and Akira.

They had watched the siege of Daraa with growing concern and then the escalation of violence across the country. They tried to live their life as normally as they could. There were power cuts and rumours of attacks, they stayed indoors in the evening but lived in fear that at any moment something terrible could happen.

The state news offered little accurate information and most of their news came from the internet and foreign news channels. They watched the trickle turn into a flood as whole families fled the conflict across Syria. They heard stories and met people fleeing atrocities.

There seems little difference in the stories about the regular army backing President Assad and those from ISIS. They understood what the Kurds were trying to achieve in northern Syria as they had always strived for independence.
.
Everyday, the news became more grim and Farid and Fatima worried every night whether they should flee to Jordan. They had heard that people were safe there. They had lost everything but were safe in Jordan, which was a little over an hour away by taxi to the south.

Farid would have to abandon his hives of bees and his home but his family's safety was surely more important. After the initial violence in 2011, the last two and a half years had been hard but they had seen little violence themselves. There were shortages and hardships for sure.

One sunny morning in 2014, Fatima took her youngest

daughter Akira to visit her sisters. Jemal and Yara went to school and Farid tended his beloved bees.

Distant gunfire suddenly broke the silence of the morning and then rockets screamed overhead and there were explosions close by and smoke and debris rising into the air. It was the start of what came to be known as the Daraa offensive.

It involved a coalition of the Free Syrian Army, the Islamic Front and the Al-Nusra Front against the Syrian Army to take over control of the south of Syria and to open up a pathway to Damascus to the east. It was the start of all out war in the south and was to have bloody consequences.

The city of Daraa was about to descend into hell that would see few buildings left intact over the next few years.

Farid hurriedly took off his overalls and headgear and ran to the school.

When he arrived the scene was chaotic. A rocket had blown up part of the school and hit two classrooms.

People were screaming and children were bleeding. He saw one man cradling a dead child in his arms. He knew the man and the child by sight but not their names. Farid was shaking with fear and he ran to the classroom that Yara was in, which had not been hit by the rocket and then ran to the classroom that Jemal sat in, which thankfully was also intact.

A neighbour walked past carrying a child, his own daughter, who was alive but covered in dust and blood. He looked over and saw four little bodies covered in blankets. He heard someone saying ' father' behind him and spun around and there was Jemal and Yara holding one another, both alive and unbloodied. He grasped them both and hugged them.

He said a silent prayer.

`We must find your mother and little sister," Farid said and then I shall return here and help.

The three of them ran from the school and headed for Fatima's sister's house. They passed one house and a shop that had been flattened to the ground and down the street that was covered in rubble and past two overturned cars. They turned the corner of the street where Fatima's sister's house was and stopped in their tracks.

Fatima's sister's house no longer existed. It had literally been blown away. They ran towards the house shouting the names of their mother and sister, Farid's throat was bone dry.

In an increasing frenzy they ran around the outside of the building until they heard a man shouting,

'Farid, Farid over here. Please come' and Farid saw that it was a neighbour of his sister in law.

'In here' he shouted and beckoned them in and there on the floor were Akira and her cousin Amira, huddled together, covered in dust and bleeding a little on the head, arms and legs. Farid bent down and hugged them both.

'They were playing in the field together with my daughter, thanks be to God, when the rocket hit the house' the neighbour explained.

Farid stood up and the neighbour put his hand on Farid's shoulder.

'Everyone in the house is dead. I am sorry. They did not stand a chance' he said. Farid thought that he was going to faint and he looked at Yara and Jemal, who had heard what the neighbour had told him. He took them both in his arms. They were starting to cry.

Instinctively they walked out into the open and walked towards the flattened house in the vain hope that perhaps the neighbour was wrong. Fatima, her sister and her husband and their son were dead.

Over the next 24 hours, Farid and others tried to find the bodies and remains of the family, which was a grim task. Then they buried the remains of his wife and her family. They did it to the background of distant gunfire and as soon as Fatima and her family were buried, Farid packed a bag and made each of the children pack a small bag also and they left.

Farid found a man who had a taxi to drive them towards the Jordanian border. After about thirty minutes, the road became clogged with vehicles and people and the driver refused to go any further. A jet roared overhead and that was it. Farid made them leave the road and they walked. That night they slept very badly in the desert.

They were cold and what little food and water they had taken with them had run out. As soon as it was dawn they started walking and the sun came up and suddenly from being cold they were hot.

Twice they flattened themselves to the ground as fighter jets flew overhead and dropped bombs in the distance. The gunfire sounded close but in all reality was probably a few miles away to the north. They walked and stopped and walked and stopped and then spent a second uncomfortable night in the desert.

On the third day they reached the Al Ramtha Border Crossing. It was utter chaos and along with what seemed like the entire population of southern Syria they walked into Jordan and slumped down exhausted.

Farid and Jemal found someone selling bottled water and bought five bottles. The rest of the day was spent queuing in the heat until they found themselves talking with a UN official.

'No' Farid had explained, 'we have no relatives in Jordan. We left Daraa after the shelling. My wife is dead and little Akiri's family are all dead. We fled for their lives.'

The official gave them some paperwork and directed them to a medical tent and then onto a food tent and were told to then join a group by the roadside and wait for a bus that would then take them to somewhere called Zaatari, which was a temporary refugee centre.

Chapter 6 - a planning proposal

The Mayor informed the Commune through his newsletter that there had been a planning permission made for the site of Guys' Cliff.

A consortium of property developers and investors wanted to create an 18 hole golf course, with a club house that incorporated health and spa facilities. What was also in the plans but not so clear was that there was also a limited number of hotel rooms with a dining facility and a business and small conference centre.

It would require an improvement in access roads and an Environmental Impact Assessment would be available on the proposal shortly. The consortium's wish was to work constructively through the good offices of the Mayor to answer any questions or concerns with the commune.

'That place has been empty for years' Arthur Barnes said, after reading the newsletter.

'With good reason' Marcel suggested as he was delivering Arthur's espresso.

'Why do you say that?' Arthur asked.

'It has, how shall we say, a troubled history" and was stopped from saying anymore as the four old fellows who met up every morning wanted a second round of Ricard.

When Marcel returned, he explained that the Mayor has organised a public meeting in the village hall (the salle de fete) in two weeks time to discuss the proposal, to meet the people behind the development and to ask questions that anyone may have.

The Mayor sent out letters to everyone and the idea of a golf club and course became the topic of conversation over those two weeks.

Chapter 7 - Zaatari

Weary and hungry, Farid with Jamil, Yara, Akira and Amira saw the temporary town of Zaatari through the windows of the bus.

Row upon row of identical tents and semi permanent buildings. It seemed to stretch for miles.

When the bus came to a halt they all climbed off and stood huddled together. They were met by UN CHF officials, who took them to a reception area. There they were offered tea and water. Farid sat them all down and they waited patiently before another official greeted them and went through the inevitable paperwork required to allow them to settle there as refugees.

It was busy and noisy and they all felt bewildered after the last few days. Farid was extremely worried about Akiri and Amira, who held hands throughout the bus journey and at the camp. They held hands tightly but the officials made no attempt to separate them. They were all too aware of the likely horrors these poor children had been through. They had seen the result of the barbarity in too many children before.

Farid explained that Jemal was his son and that Yara and Akira were his daughters and that Amari was his niece who had seen her entire family blown up in a rocket attack along with his own wife Fatima.

A kindly Jordanian woman explained that they were joining a very large extended family of some 80,000 fellow Syrians who have been forced to flee the war in Syria. Zaatari was in northern Jordan and they would be safe there. More than half of everyone there were children. Since 2012 the camp, divided into 12 districts, has grown from a collection of tents to a semi-permanent city.

She saw Farid with tears of relief in his eyes and rubbed his shoulder. She knew that with the conflict in the south of Syria that number was likely to swell by up to 150,000 Syrian refugees.

She had smiled and said that Zaatari was now the fourth-largest city in Jordan.

When they finished their tea, she took them to a prefabricated shelter. The prefabricated shelter had just been erected to replace some of the tents. It was to be their new home, that had been allocated to them. It was kitted out with bedding, a simple cooking stove and toiletries and towels.

She then apologised, saying that she had more new arrivals to attend to but that their new neighbours would show them where all the other facilities were such as toilets and showers, the canteens and the communal meeting places were and where to find some new clothes.

They were all exhausted and within the hour all four children were asleep. Farid sat looking at them and only then did he allow himself to begin to sob, his chest heaving. He had tried to remain strong for the entire week that it had taken them to arrive at Zaatari.

In fear for his children and his niece, he had had no time to mourn his wife's death. His relief that he had got his children here and that they were now alive and safe, was mixed with his utter sadness and despair at Fatima and Fatima's whole family's death. He suddenly felt overwhelmed and in the darkness of their new home he cried into the night until sleep stole away his complete sadness.

After a few weeks in their new city of Zaatari, Jemal settled in well in and was a popular boy in their part of the makeshift town.

Jemal had played football in Syria for his school team

before the war. He loved football and would watch European football games on the TV dreaming that one day he would be playing football for one of the big teams.

Now Jemal had joined men and children inside the camp to play football on the streets and with younger children in the playground. He had then progressed to the football field on the edge of the camp.

It was from playing football that he had been spotted as a potential talent and was invited to train with Mansheyat Bani Hasan, a football club who were in the second division of the Jordanian football league. It was then that he was invited to be a coach himself in Zaatari

Jemal turned 18 in 2016 and became a football coach for girl's football. Girls football was being developed under UNICEF's Makani football initiative. Makani means 'Myspace' in Arabic. The centre in Zaatari provided a safe space for youths to access learning opportunities and build life skills, especially young girls. They studied and were taught a range of skills to encourage them to become independent and able to work.

To everyone's surprise playing football gathered momentum for the girls who refused to believe that it was a game just for boys and so football flourished, it was a physical outlet and it gave them all enormous confidence to be seen as equals to the boys. Jemal felt very honoured to be asked to have such a role as their coach.

Jemal loved it. He also studied when he was not coaching or playing, which was most of the time.

Yara wanted to go to Europe. She wanted to work in fashion, to combine traditional Arabic dress with western fashion. So she started to take the opportunity in Zaatari to learn about fabric and to assist in the clothes bank in the refugee camp and became active in trying to promote Zaatari with European companies, who could support the refugees with clothing.

Akira and Amira did not integrate quickly. They needed a lot of psychological support and were reluctant to leave Farid's side at first. When they had first arrived in Zaatari they jumped at any loud noises and stuck together nearly all the time. They attended school and sat next to one another. Over time they started to relax but always kept that closeness. Yara and Jemal would take turns to send time with them when their father needed a break.

Yara and Jemal also befriended a young man called Ibrahim. Ibrahim had fled from the north. He was Kurdish by birth and had been fleeing from ISIS with his family and they had tried to reach Turkey. It was here that the Turkish army took a stand against the Kurds, fearful that the Kurds in Turkey would form an alliance with the Syrian Kurds.

The fighting had been brutal and Ibrahim had seen his father and older brother killed in fighting and his mother had died of an infection from a shrapnel wound. Over the next two months Ibrahim had wandered south until he found a small convoy of people heading for Jordan and he had hitched a ride but not before one of the cars had been shot to pieces and everyone killed inside by a group of ISIS fighters.

Ibrahim had arrived in Zaatari alone. He had been badly traumatised at the death and destruction that he had experienced. In addition, he had been wounded in the fighting and had had shrapnel removed from his leg when he arrived in Zaatari. When Yara and Jemal told their Father about his story, Farid went and saw him and asked that he come and work with him on the water recycling plant that he was helping with.

From there he invited Ibrahim to eat with them and asked permission that he join them where they were living.

'No one should be alone in this world and this boy has lost everything' was his plea to the authorities who ran the camp and they would not disagree, so Ibrahim came to live with them.

Chapter 8 - The public meeting

The Mayor welcomed everyone to a very packed meeting and with little formality thanked Mr Julian Castide for coming to the meeting and invited him to speak.

Julian Castide stood up and threw his arms wide open and said hello. He spoke slowly and melodically. He walked along the front of the room and along the side, walking closely to those he was speaking to.

'Thank you to the Mayor and the Commune for giving me the time and space to talk with you. I especially want to thank you all for taking the time to come here and see for yourselves just what we are trying to achieve here. All around the walls you can see photographs and information on the benefits of a development like this'.

You could have heard a pin drop. He held the audience immediately. He was almost mesmeric. Some later admitted that it felt like they were in the presence of a healer or spiritual leader. His words seem to speak directly and personally to each and every person in the room.

He made the joke about the fact that for some golf spoiled a nice walk in the country. He said that he could not play golf very well himself but it freed up many women's and a few men's lives to have their husbands and wives to go and play this game and give them some peace and quiet, with the added bonus that they usually came back happy.

The villagers had smiled and some had laughed and he stood there looking at each and everyone of them, with eye contact.

Beautifully coiffured and with a slight sun tan he continued.

'So, firstly what are Golf's Environmental Opportunities? We have environmental partners who we work closely with giving us both sound education and technical assistance. It is a fact, often forgotten that golf courses are uniquely positioned to offer a host of environmental benefits.'

'They provide much needed wildlife sanctuaries and they preserve natural areas and support plants and wildlife native to the area. It is a well known fact that now because of their design they protect water resources. They filter storm water run off through golf course wetlands and turf grass and they rehabilitate degraded landscapes.'

'Then there are the human factors - they promote physical and mental well being which reduces stress and they Improve air quality and moderate temperature. Just being a member of the club helps promote and educate both the golfers and the general public about the nature of the game and promote environmentally-sound management of the environment. It is a feel good factor all around.'

'A well run Golf Club brings a good image and reputation: It will enhance the good name of this fine village.'

'Then there are the economic benefits to the commune. We will increase the income to the commune from the business charges, it will create employment for local people in the running of the golf course and its facilities. It will bring additional business to local traders here.'

'Customer satisfaction is also an added improvement. The creation of this course will enrich golfers' experience of the game. I am now going to quote from a number of surveys - have shown that golfers report that playing quality is maintained or even improved as a result of steps taken to manage a course in harmony with the natural environment.'

'I would now like to invite you to have complimentary drinks from us and to walk and look around the information that we have provided and to talk with myself and my two partners here. We prefer the informal approach as experience teaches us that this is more helpful. Thank you.'

And with that Julian Castide sat down and the caterers took to their feet and started to serve drinks.

Julian Castide was suave and professional and he was very handsome. He had piercing dark blue eyes, almost black and he spoke in a melodic and entrancing manner. There were a number of women who were already swooning, a couple transfixed in their seats as if they still could hear his voice.

'If that man was an ice cream, he'd lick himself' Jean Paul whispered to me in my ear.

I watched him over the next thirty minutes work the room and then the caterers started to clear up. The big sell was timed to perfection and would soon be over. Everyone had had a couple of drinks and some petite fours and were happy. Julian Castide reminded me of a mix of the old style faith healers and preachers in terms of rhetoric wrapped in a trained politician's cover, with the suit to match.

Lucille, the journalist from Quest France, had been listening in the audience and taking notes. She walked over to Julian Castide and introduced herself.

'Enchante' he said and kissed her on both cheeks, 'how good to meet you and thank you for coming to listen'.

'It's an ambitious and interesting development Mr Castide. I wanted to ask you a few questions if that is OK as I want to do a piece for the newspaper' She asked.

'Listen, why don't we meet for lunch and that will give us more time. There are a lot of people that I should say hello to here at the moment? I am staying in Dinan for the next two days in a hotel by the river down in the port. How about tomorrow at 12.30?

'Perfect'

'My assistant over there has the address of the hotel' he said pointing to an equally snappily dressed young man.

'No mention of the environmental impact on building it then' Gerard said to me.

'And not one mention of a pesticide either' Jean Paul added. I looked over at the Mayor, who looked anxious after talking with the Professor.

The Professor had walked over to talk to Julian Castide,

'Your presentation was very optimistic might I say, Mr Castide' the Professor started, 'but as I am sure that you are aware, the reason why there are now Environmental Impact Assessments required on golf courses is because environmentalists have long argued that the land used for golf courses are not only a waste of space, but also do great damage to the environment, especially with the large scale use pesticides and watering, which destroys habitats for wildlife species.'

'My dear fellow, you are absolutely correct in what you say but a little bit behind the times, if I may say' Julian Castide responded.

Undeterred, the Professor continued.

'Then there is the construction and operation of these golf courses. There are practices that can be extremely harmful to the environment, clearing the natural habitat, the pollution of the soil from not just pesticides but fertilisers and herbicides and sometimes even hormones, which are the plant stimulants to speed up growth.'

' As I said, perhaps a little bit behind the times. New research and new science has virtually eliminated these issues. You are referring to very outdated products' he replied smoothly.

'Well it has not worked with farming that brilliantly yet has it, we still have terrible runoffs into the rivers' said the Professor.

'Well that is the struggle between politicians, the farming interests and the environmentalists. All we do is learn from them and not make the same mistakes. It has been a pleasure talking with you' and with that Julian Castide was gone.

'Not such a good conversation then Professor?' Jean Paul said.

'Too smooth and slick for me I'm afraid' he said.

'Smooth, smart and a shit' would be my summary for what it is worth' Jean Paul shrugged.

'All my academic learning and lifetime of reading and you sum it up expertly in five words'. The Professor smiled.

'And that was Jean Paul being diplomatic,' the Mayor said.

Chapter 9 - Ryan and Rose Marie O'Keefe

Farid remained the rock to the five young people now under his charge and he devoted most of his time to being there for them.

He had also become involved in the water projects that became essential for Zaatari to function as an isolated city with so many people living in it. The recycling plant was run by the UN and it was here that he met Ryan O'Keefe, an Irish man who worked as a water engineer with the UN.

Over six months Farid and Ryan became friends and Farid had invited Ryan to meet his family and Ryan had invited Farid and his family to meet his French wife Rose Marie. They had cooked dinner for them.

About one month after that dinner, Rose Marie and Ryan sat down one evening to discuss their own plans.

'You are due to sign a contract for another three years next month. Is that what you want to do?' She had asked.

Ryan looked at her. 'Honest answer is yes, I feel that my work here is half done and that the projects that are being developed will be nearly completed by that time. The question of me is do you want to continue here for another three years?

Rose Marie worked for an NGO, a non governmental organisation and her work was in developing skills and qualifications for women in the camp. This ranged from education to business studies, to developing greenhouses for food for the camp and teaching market gardening. She was also involved in trying to develop links with middle eastern and European countries to create work opportunities.

Of all the refugees in the camp, the majority of adults were women and most had not worked before the war.'

'I love what I am doing here. Of course I want to stay'. She had answered immediately.

'But we have a house in France which we have not visited in a year and the year before that we went there once, for a week'. Ryan said, knowing full well that when they had taken leave it was easier to go to Egypt for a break and they also often cannot visit in the months between May and September because they rent the house out to tourists.

'I've been thinking,' Ryan started.

'Oh no' Rose Marie said laughing, 'what now?'

``We should rent the house out long term rather than holiday lets' He suggested.

'Why?' Rose Marie asked, 'the rentals bring in a good amount of money and Linda looks after the house well and Jean Paul, the garden'.

'I think we should let the house out to a refugee family here in Zaatari. A family that wants to resettle in France. With us sponsoring them and their accommodation provided, that would tick plenty of boxes in the asylum application'. He expanded.

'The house has no mortgage. Sure the rentals pay for the local taxes and bills and upkeep and leave some pocket money but we do not really need it. We are both working and about to commit to another three years here, so?' He concluded by opening his arms in an accompanying gesture.

'And you have someone in mind I suppose?'

'As a matter of fact, yes, I do. I have said nothing to them because I wanted to talk with you first.'

'The Khalil's?' She asked.

'Yes' He responded.

'OK' She replied. 'Talk me through why?'

'Well, Farid is a farmer, well a beekeeper by trade but he also has good engineering and general farming knowledge. Although they came from Daraa, they have more of a rural background than an urban one. The two little girls need tranquility and peace, not a noisy city.

Jemal and Yara would thrive in France and both probably obtain apprenticeships and with us sponsoring them, then hopefully we can argue that Farid can take Ibrahim also, who is now 17 and has no family except the Khalils'

'Brilliant. I agree,' Rose Marie said.

'You do?'

'I do'.

Rose Marie stood up and went to the kitchen and put water in the kettle.

'However, there is one flaw in the plan. Ibrahim will not be counted as family for the qualification criteria. We would need to adopt him. You and I. Then he would become a French citizen through me and would be able to travel to his new home and have Farid and the family accompany him'.

'Wow' said Ryan. 'You'd do that?'

`If you will,' she replied.

'I love you Rose Marie. Marrying you was the best thing that I ever did.'

'And this is the best thing that we have ever done between us.'

The next day, Rose Marie and Ryan made their enquiries and talked with colleagues in the camp who would advise them of the process and what needed to be done.

In a nutshell, the word was bureaucracy and how to wade through it.

Ryan and Rose Marie also sat down with Farid to talk to him about what they were proposing. When they told him, Farid cried for only a second time in five years. The fact that they wanted to include Ibrahim also needed to be talked through as Farid already had four children to look after but he was delighted.

None of them had any paperwork in relation to identification save what was provided to them through the UN and the Jordanian authorities.

The criteria for granting asylum were in a nutshell legal and/or physical protection needs survivors of violence and/or torture, medical needs, women and girls at risk, family reunification, children and adolescents at risk and lack of foreseeable alternative durable solutions.

A number of those criteria had applied to them all in order to have refugee status in Jordan and now the war still showed no sign of ending. The ability to return to their old home was not an option as it no longer existed and the beehives would have been burnt by those who did stay for firewood.

When Farid explained what the O'Keefes were proposing the children all loved the idea. France was somewhere where they could only dream of and Ibrahim could not believe that anyone would want to be so kind. He could not believe the kindness of Farid and how he treated him as an equal to his own children and his niece and now this.

His family, his mother, father and little sister were dead in unmarked graves somewhere in Syria, murdered by a killer from the sky. Someone trained to fly planes and drop bombs and was paid to do this as a living. Someone who had dropped bombs on a civilian area in the full knowledge that there were women and children below. People who had been defenceless and were now dead or maimed.

He had spent months angry and frightened and slowly with Farid and his family, his anger had subsided, his loneliness and loss had drifted away in the love of this man and his family.

Over the next six months of paperwork, wrangling and arguing with different departments, they succeeded.

They were a success story of all the energy that the people of Jordan, the NGO's and UN officials had put into Zaatari.

When they had booked their flights from Amman to Paris, they all went to say goodbye to friends that they had made and also asked if the O'Keefe's could arrange a thank you party for their colleagues who had helped and supported them after the worst days of their lives.

For all the Khalil's, it was their first time ever in a plane and they all crowded around the window seat to look out and below them. Marie Rose travelled with them to ensure their reception into France went as smooth as possible and to take them to their house. They landed in Paris with her. There they were met by Ryan had hired a minibus from the airport to their house in France.

When they climbed out of the minibus, Linda and Jean Paul (who had gone round to Linda's at 11.00 am to make sure that she was up) met them having prepared the house and made the beds and cut the grass the day before.

Rose Marie turned to Farid, Yara, Amira and Akira, Jemal and Ibrahim.

'Welcome to La Croix de Bois'

When they arrived in France, the Syrian Civil War was in its eighth year between four main warring factions of ISIS, Kurdish forces, the Assad government, and other opposition groups and bombing from Russian and Turkish forces.

In that time, the conflict had led to more than 500,000 deaths. It is estimated that it displaced over half of Syria's population with 6.2 million Syrians internally displaced, and 5.6 million are refugees, predominantly in Lebanon,

Jordan, and Turkey. Jordan alone is estimated to have taken more than double its existing population.

Chapter 10 - The Professor explains

The Professor and I had met up walking around the lake as he was keen to tell me more about Guy's Cliff, the foreboding and sad looking house and estate overlooking the river on a cliff, hence its name Guy's Cliff.

The Professor, like everyone else, could not say why it was called Guy's cliff as no-one seemed to know who Guy was but it was certainly perched on a cliff.

'The last incumbent Tomas De Vere, died in 1978 at the age of 74' the Professor started 'and had been a near recluse from after the second World War. His wife had tragically hanged herself in 1947 and Tomas never seemed to recover. He had inherited the house at the age of 22 in 1926 following the death of his Father.

'Around that time there were all kinds of stories about black magic and a group of people who used to meet at the house to practice certain forms of the occult. The story has it that they were trying to conjure up a demon to control a book called an Agrippa.'

'A demon to control a book?' I had asked.

'Yes, a book. They were called Grimoires. In the sixteenth and seventeenth centuries many books were written about occult practices covering potions and natural science and spells, rituals and so forth. They were referred to as Grimoires. Indeed there is even a notorious one supposedly written by Pope Honorius' The Professor continued.

'A Grimoire written by the Pope?

'Attributed to the Pope. The Grimoire of Pope Honorius is the first and most important of the French 'black magic' Grimoires. It contains ways to summon demons, a number of simple charms for health, for wealth, for sex and for ways to protect oneself and a book of certain secrets. It was said to be second only to the Grimoire called the Key of Solomon, in how it influenced magicians and priests in France. Jean Paul would refer to them as con men and he would probably be right.

It became notorious because its use was involved in a scandal that rocked the Royal Court in 1679 known as the Affair of Poisons'.

'The affair of poisons' I repeated.

'Yes, the affair of poisons. Here look,' the Professor said, handing me his lap top. This is what Wikipeadia says

I read it - *The Affair of Poisons (l'affaire des poisons) was a major murder scandal in France during the reign of King Louis XIV.Between 1677 and 1682, a number of prominent members of the aristocracy were implicated and sentenced on charges of poisoning and witchcraft The scandal reached into the inner circle of the king. It led to the execution of 36 people.*

I handed back the Professor's laptop to him.

'And again it was involved in the murder of an archbishop by a young priest in 1857.'

This was turning into some history lesson and all this from a book.

'Now the Grimoire of Honorius also referred to another Grimoire called the Agrippa the Professor started, 'the Agrippa is in another league to anything else. Simply put, it is the book that does not want to die.

It was named after a man called Heinrich Agrippa sometime in the 16th Century. He wrote three books on the occult about the relationship between natural and ritual magic mixed in with the religions of the times.

There was a fourth book attributed to him after he had died, which went much further about the summoning of demons and spirits. Now this book was believed to have been alive and when not being used had to be locked with a padlock and chained to something secure in the house so that it could not be moved.'

The Professor had my interest. I was captivated.

'It was said to be written by the devil himself but of course the number of copies that were around would have kept him busy full time, so that is yet another myth that is around this book.

The book was claimed to be able to predict the future. The book itself could only be handled by priests specifically trained to use it and strong enough to control it mentally.'

I sat silently listening to this knowledgeable man.

'Apparently one version states that it was written in blood, the devil's blood; the other that it was black pages that only an Initiate could see and read. These Initiates were originally trained and taught at a famous seminary in Quimper.

There was a belief that Initiate priests could control the weather through this book, summon demons to find out what had happened to dead relatives in terms of going to hell or heaven and even predict future happenings.

All this from the book, not the devil or from God but from the written word or blank page. In Brittany these priests became known as the Fizikars and were seen as sorcerers. I would imagine that Breton history has intermingled this with the Pagans of old'.

I uninterrupted the Professor.

'For a book, it seems to have an amazing amount of power' I suggested.

'In the right hands, of course it does. If you believe that the book has truth then it becomes powerful. Consider the Bible or Koran. To you and me it is a collection of stories and tales and at times not very well written and inconsistent, cobbled together from different texts.

To a believer they are two of the most powerful books on earth that people believe in every word and are ruled by their texts. People's very lives depend on their interpretations.' He suggested.

It was true, I guess, a book of simple spells and potions, on how to summon spirits was small fry compared to the Bible and Koran. People have killed and been killed over the Bible and the Koran, so something called a Grimoire or the Agrippa might sound supernatural but in the hands of a believer, then it was powerful stuff.

The Professor stopped walking for a moment.

'Then came the Revolution. Thousands of priests were forced out of their comfortable lives as the people rebelled against the religious dominance of their lives along with the aristocracy and king.'

'So these Agrippas apparently disappeared or were destroyed but others fell into the hands of the layman, untrained persons, who were fascinated by these Tomes but who could not control the forces of the book either physically or mentally.

Legend has it that the Priests knew when to stop reading the book. They were trained to know when to stop so that it never took control but not the layman and therefore havoc and mayhem was the result for those foolish to become involved.'

'So you can see the power such a book could invoke to

those who wanted to believe it. Why am I telling you all this? Because it is believed that there was a copy of the Agrippa in Guys' Cliff and that it was used with terrifying consequences.'

'One of the myths associated with the legends is that anyone who uses it runs the risk of great and continual pain.'

'Why?'

'Because of the contact with the devil but this pain was perfectly acceptable given the powers that could be invoked' the Professor answered.

'So what happened?' I asked.

'It is hard to know apart from the stories we are told. Before Tomas inherited the house there were stories of a person throwing themselves from the cliff into the river. A fire that destroyed part of one end of the house and that two people died in that fire unable to escape. Now what is interesting about this story is that legend has it that the Agrippa can only be destroyed with fire, so who knows'.

'I am telling you all this about Agrippa as a background. Guys' Cliff has had a terrible and frightful history from when it was built to this very day.' Then the Professor stopped and looked at me.

'I have known you long enough that you understand the history around these parts of the thin veil between the present and the past or the natural and the supernatural, or the living and the dead, however you want to describe it. It is a gift and can be a curse like everything from money to faith to hope. I know what you see.'

'There is a power in La Croix de Bois that makes us all better people. I know it but I do not understand it and I do not want to understand it. It is a gift and it needs to always be protected.'

I explained that I knew some of the popular history of Guys' Cliff that and sunk into folklore or popular story but not what the Professor was telling me.

'But Guys' Cliff is different' the Professor continued. 'It is not a bad place but it is a sad place and it has a terrible history, especially as it sits so close to here.'

'The time has come that we must do something to reverse that. After Tomas de Vere died in 1978, it lay empty for 6 years and then it was bought to be run as a hotel and over the next 6 years it ran as a failing hotel.'

'Guests are said to have left terrified in the night because of noises and things moving and staff had to be employed from far away as local people would not work there especially at night. In 1992 it closed its doors and has been empty ever since.'

'Like all these strange occurrences - are they real? Did the guest really experience these things? Or has the history and story telling of Guys' Cliff turned imaginations.'

'Perhaps Guys' Cliff is a bad place after all, or as I said a sad place that has had bad people living there, or not bad people but people committed to beliefs that are of an occult nature.'

'For many followers of the occult it is a type of religion and belief system that should do no harm and invoke good things but it is surrounded in practices that others interpret as evil.'

'Perhaps in modern parlance, just like pagan practices, they are now seen as unchristian, the worship of false gods that were at times sexually riven, which, in their day were seen as perfectly normal practices.'

'Within any group or sect there are those who use religious

and spiritual practices and writings for their own ends. It is why Europe and the Middle East has torn itself apart for thousands of years with religious bigotry. Occultists are no different.'

'At the end of the day they, like us' are human beings, complete with all their mental frailties and desires, their bigotries and their self beliefs.'

'Now there is a consortium who want to buy it and run it as a hotel-come golf club and to redevelop the 81 hectares into a golf course. It must be stopped because it is my belief that the combination of the history and the creation of a golf course and all that this will bring will have very bad consequences for La Croix de Bois and for all of us'.

'Whatever you believe, it is my feeling that Guy's Cliff has a long history of trying to summon demons and maybe even the worship of such ideas as the devil. Sometimes such places develop an energy or mystic about them that enables men and women to damn themselves'.

'I have heard it said that perhaps such places should be erased from the earth along with the antiquated beliefs of hell and damnation that surround it. I have been on this earth for a very long time and now sometimes I confuse myself. We should finish our walk and go and let me buy you a drink and talk of kinder and more pleasant things' the Professor concluded.

We walked around the remaining part of the lake and into the village, in relative silence. After such considerations, small talk about life in the village seemed a little strange in itself.

Chapter 11 - Karen and Alain Dupont, the Organic Farmers

I had the good fortune to be introduced to Karen and Alain Dupont by Jean Paul. They were running a small farm outside of the village. It was relatively small scale but produced enough for them to run a stall for organic vegetables and fruit in La Croix de Bois on market day and three other local markets.

They had invited Jean Paul to join them for a picnic by the lake and Karen's parents were going to be with them then they thought that it would be a good opportunity for Jean Paul to see them as they had known him for forty or fifty years. They had not really been friends with Jean Paul, more acquaintancies and on the rare occasion that they met, then they would always stop and exchange pleasantries.

Jean Paul invited me to join them and I was happy to do so and bought with me more bread and cheese, some olives and of course some pate.

We were sitting on the bank of the lake and Karen and Alain had bought four fold up chairs for the 'pensioners' which was thoughtful. French picnics involved chairs and fold up tables, picnic hampers and wine from the bottle with coolers and a blanket on the ground.

Jean Paul and the parents, Yves Johan and Sylvie, ran through all the people they knew jointly, who had had what operation, everyone's health, who had died and who had had children. The normal things people do when they have a lot of catching up to do and then we found ourselves talking about the state of the world and of course organic farming.

The stall on the market had grown great support over the last three years and villagers even bought their brown paper bags back week after week to hold the latest purchases. Their stall was not the pristine regular shaped vegetables, the carrots not so bright orange, the eggs different sizes and colour but everyone seemed to love them.

Yves Johan poured us all a glass of wine,

'I want to toast my daughter and son-in-law', he started, 'for what they are trying to do. Sylvie and I are old. Old socialists, farmers of the land, believers still in the commune and a French way of life that we see changing almost daily, just like most of the world is changing. Some of it is good but some of it not'.

' Brittany is part of France and France is part of Europe and in truth is better for it. In many ways it has bought investment and prosperity to the poorer regions and countries of Europe and it has certainly brought us all closer together which is the most important thing' he stated, 'but before the common agricultural policy, most farms in Brittany were 80% self sufficient and the remaining 20% they bartered and exchanged between farms and these farms had enough of what they produced to feed their local hamlets and villages.'

'The farms were supported by people like blacksmiths and coopers and so forth. Don't get me wrong. It was not the idyllic lifestyle we all make it out to be. None of us were rich but no one starved.'

'The Common Agricultural policy meant that all farmers were supported or subsidised if you like, in order to produce food. The new emerging Europe needed to have its shops full of produce when the eastern bloc was struggling big time to achieve this and the propaganda on this was enormous.'

'But for the farmers to achieve this, then they needed to modernise and combine their small farms into larger ones. Then with bigger fields, you needed bigger machines for ploughing and harvesting. The dairy and pig farms grew. Now, to maintain a herd of cows that are fifty or more takes an enormous amount of land and shelter and in the winter a lot of feed.'

'The pig farms are no longer small styes and enclosures with five to ten pigs but they have became industrialised, into large scale indoor buildings. For chickens it was the same moving from a small shed and coops to huge hangers. Not necessarily battery style farms but huge indoor barns. The difference between fresh air eggs and free range was an argument that had become passionate.

So the farms grew bigger and the farming communes became stimulated by the businesses that produced combine harvesters and tractors and a whole range of mechanised products. The fields had had their natural fabric of trees torn down to make ploughing simpler and more economical, but then the earth needed to be better fertilised and protected from wind erosion and general degradation.

It is the same story as ever. The farmers can only exist on subsidies and the growth of large scale supermarkets meant that they very quickly controlled the market price, often selling cheap products that never reflected the true costs for the farmers. So the pressure was always on to increase yields, so in came the pharmaceuticals with their - hormones and injections for livestock, fertilisers and growing products for the crops. Yields greatly increased and then we started to complain about our rivers and our drinking water because the run off from all this innovation went straight into our rivers and then into the sea'.

Yves Johan looked at us all.

Sorry I am going on' he said.

'Yes you are Dad', Karen said

'He could not be any different' Sylvie laughed', 'and if he was then I would not love him like I do'

'I do not have the answers' Yves Johann continued, 'but what my daughter and son in law are trying to do, I fully support. The mess we have reached suits the businessmen from supermarket chains to the pharmaceutical companies to the vehicle industry. Do they suit us? Who can say'.

'Some things are changing but it is on a small scale. The consumer will always be driven by price ultimately. If they can afford free range or wild fish or organically grown vegetables they will but when the mass produced equivalent is half the price or less for many then that is no competition.'

Yves Johann stopped talking and ate some bread and cheese.

Jean Paul decided to join in.

'Did you know that the average lifespan of a chicken is between 40 and 48 days, and most dairy cows, because of intensive milking, die at an early age. Most beef comes from heifers that live only for two years.'

'We know these facts, we see the pigs being transported to the slaughter houses and we do not like it but we still go and buy the pork because it is on special offer.' Karen added.

'And when you can have cheap red and green peppers flown up from Spain in the middle of winter and they cost less than a locally grown cabbage then the world has lost all sense.' Jean Paul added.

Yves Johann climbed to his feet and went to the car and returned with another bottle of red wine and a bottle of white wine. 'These bottles are not organic but they are bloody cheap,' and he started laughing and we all joined him in a chortle.

'Before I depress you anymore let us drink' he said.

'The world will never be dull while there is wine in it' Yves Johan concluded.

Chapter 12 - the interview

Lucille made sure that she was on time for her interview. As she approached the reception desk, she saw that Julian Castide was already sitting in the foyer.

He stood up and smiled at her.

'Shall we have a drink before we eat?' He suggested and they walked over to the bar. Lucille ordered a small white wine and he did the same.

The waiter brought the menu to them while they sipped their wine and Lucille asked Julian about the development and then about the man himself.

'I am from a very normal and ordinary background, all very unremarkable. No sob stories or childhood traumas. I did all the usual things growing up on the outskirts of Tours and then when I went to Paris. That is when my life definitely took off and I met some quite extraordinary people.'

Over lunch they talked about a range of things from business concepts and how to develop projects, to art and books and the world.

Lucille was fascinated by the man and found herself slightly mesmerised. His intellectual knowledge and reading was extensive. He recounted anecdotes but asked more questions of her and paid attention to her answers. Lucille was normally used to men talking about themselves but Julian asked about her and her thoughts on issues and what it was like to work on a regional newspaper, he asked about her background and her personal interests.

They had ordered a bottle of wine between them and the plat du jour which ran to three courses. Lucille felt like she was falling in love with this man. She had never met anyone like him before. He was charming her.

Instead of interviewing him, she was telling him about her relationship with her boyfriend and how it was going nowhere. It was not horrible but it lost its sparkle and was dull and now they were going through the motions. She was sitting there telling this stranger intimate things about her life. How was this happening?

When they finished their meal, he suggested that they go and sit on his terraced balcony overlooking the river for a coffee. Lucille tried to feign uncertainty and looked at her watch, as a poor attempt to not say yes immediately.

When she walked into his room, her heart was thumping in her chest. His room was large and the terrace had, as he had said a beautiful view along the river Rance. He had clearly booked one of the best rooms.

As they sat there with their coffee looking at one another and across the river, she hardly heard a word he was saying. Five minutes later, Lucille found herself totally naked after walking into the room from the terrace and slipping off her dress and underwear in front of him, without any inhibition. He had asked her to that very thing and she had. She had almost obeyed him but done so willingly.

Then she had lain on the bed and watched him slowly undress himself before her.

Lucille could not believe what was happening. She knew that it was all real but had a dreamlike quality to it. She had a kind of far away feeling. She had been totally seduced by this man and was loving it. Her head was swimming.

Then came the sex. It was fantastic. Julian Castide did things to her, with her that she had literally never done before and she was letting him and she felt wild. The afternoon seemed to disappear and time became irrelevant.

When they finally came to a halt, every bit of her tingled. He ordered room service and they drank more coffee and orange juice on the terrace and Lucille had to leave and Julian had a business appointment.

As Lucille drove home, she was still in a trance and was still tingling and certain parts of her were still throbbing even when she arrived home. The article she had to write would have to wait until tomorrow.

Julian was pleased with how lunch and the afternoon had gone. It was important to have the journalist onside. She had been a pleasant distraction. He had had to tone down his usual sexual proclivities with her but that was OK. For Julian Castide, it was all in a day's work.

She had been putty in his hand and they always were, normally. He also contented himself with Lucille that he knew that he had saved her. He had saved her from a relationship that she would have continued putting energy into which was already doomed. Better that she ended it sooner rather than later. In addition to ensuring that Lucille would give him a good write up, how could she not, it also gave him righteous justification for his seduction. As his mother had always stated – he was a saviour.

Chapter 13 - the post office and the tourists

I have just bumped into Madeline and Giles Pertwee. They have just spent twenty five minutes queuing at the post office. Actually, the post office in the village is a room. The room is located within the Mayor's building located next to the reception area where the secretary and the administrator sit.

They had been trying to collect a letter sent to them last week. The 'you were absent' note was dated for the Thursday so collection would be the day afterwards but the Friday was a bank holiday and was therefore closed. It was also closed over the weekend. On the Monday, the administrator was off sick, so as the notice stated, due to exceptional circumstances the post room was closed. Tuesday morning the post room was always closed and Tuesday afternoon Giles had a hospital appointment, so finally on Wednesday morning, they had their letter and walked away with a sense of having overcome great adversity.

The post room is locked but the rest of the Mayor's building is open. The Mairie (Mayor's building) is open Monday to Friday from 09.00 to 12.00 and from 14.00 to 17.00. The post room is not. It is open on Monday, Wednesday and

Friday mornings between 09.00 and 12.00. It is also open on Tuesday, Thursday and Friday afternoons between 14.00 and 17.00. On Thursday it is closed.

Turn up on the wrong day to collect a letter or parcel that needed to be signed for that the post man or woman could not deliver, and no manner of persuading or pleading could make neither the secretary nor administrator get up from their desk and go and unlock the post room. That was the rule and rules cannot be broken.

The receipt for collection also had a time when it would be available 24 hours from when the failed delivery took place. Even if the post room was unlocked and open but the 24 hours had not elapsed then neither the secretary nor the administrator would look for it, even though it might be there. That was the rule and rules were not to be broken.

Once you accepted this was the situation and the rules were the rules and had served the commune well for decades, then everything was fine.

The Tourist season is also beginning to start with a vengeance and this made additional planning necessary. As a local you learn that from the beginning of July, you had to get up an hour earlier if you wanted fresh bread from the boulangerie before the horde of tourists descended on the boulangerie and then onto the supermarket for cheese, because that is another rule as a tourist – a holiday in France always means fresh bread and cheese.

Many a tourist can be seen strutting along the pavement with a baguette tucked under their arm believing that they were now officially French.

The other 'rules' were - forget parking in the square as it would always be heaving with cars, and if you wanted to eat out any evening book the restaurant at least two days in advance. A stroll along the river or around the lake was likely to involve at least twenty other parties of dog walkers.

Always stop at junctions. The local traffic rules allowed anyone coming out of a road on the right direct access onto the main road. This had been a little troubling to start with but was now adopted by everyone as courteous and accepted practice. Tourists and especially foreign tourists were not psychic and neither did they have any road signs to give them a clue as to this expected practice.

As a result the whole of July and August was one long series of near accidents from someone pulling out from the right onto a main road. This was a clear proceedure backed up either with a solid white line, in which case the person coming from the right had to stop but with no white line, they were perfectly entitled to sail right out.

A fact known and respected most of the time locally, it was an alien concept to visitors and tourists. The outcome was cars on the main road would suddenly break unexpectedly, with the result that the car behind would have to break even harder, because someone had just pulled out in front of them without warning and the person behind, who was naturally tail gating, which is a common French national pastime and right of passage, then having to slam their brakes on as they have left so little space for an emergency stop.

Other than that, the tourists are welcomed as they bring in much needed income. The second homers all return and usually eat in the local restaurants and there is a general feel good atmosphere to the entire village. Just enough visitors but not too many. The ubiquitous curse for many places these days is the crush of tourists, whose momentum seems to change the type of shops that appear, and a change in the atmosphere and mood of the town or village.

La Croix de Bois has just about got that balance right. It was a concern that the last thing the village needed was a new large planning proposal.

Chapter 14 - the man behind the plan

So, who is Julien Castide and what does he represent?.

Two days after attending the public meeting in La Croix de Bois, Julian Castide was sitting on his large white leather sofa finishing a telephone call.

'As I said, the meeting was attended by the usual collection of villagers, half concerned and half with euro signs flashing in their heads. One or two people there might cause a little trouble if they are allowed to, but with the department of the Cotes d'Armor onboard and the key people we have 'persuaded' at the regional level within Brittany, on our side then I think it is fairly much in the bag. Hopefully we can start to develop the site in the next couple of months. OK?' and he pressed the red button on the mobile and ended the call.

Julian Castide was excited. The development of Guys' Cliff gave him a base in Brittany to further both his business influence but also his more esoteric and occult practices, in addition to his psychological and hypnotic skills. Practices that had made him a richer and a more influential man, just as the books had said. He had read the Grimoire of Honorius and it had given him exactly what it said on the cover.

I conjure thee, Oh book to be useful and profitable unto all those who shall read thee for success in their affairs.'

And it worked. He had read and learned the book, he had learned and practiced hypnosis, studied psychology, looked at how the behavioural sciences operated in the commercial sector. He was a profound fan of the so-called 'nudge theory' which was the art of making people do things that they were not contemplating but did so by small incremental steps that they were often unaware of and which they considered were positive.

On top of that, he was well educated and undeniably good looking. Not just good looking but drop dead handsome. He knew it and so did everyone he met. In addition, he paid people attention when he needed to before discarding them if they were no longer useful. There was nothing complicated about that. People yearned for attention – to be listened to, to be looked at, to be paid compliments. It cost him nothing apart from a little time and it bought him what he wanted.

Of course to back all that, money also helped. At times it was the greatest influence in the art of persuasion. For Julian Castide, the acquisition of money for himself, and lots of it took was the priority but t never hurt to let other people and other companies to cash in alongside him.

The golf course development had the backing of certain interests and elements that he considered rather distasteful himself but the indulgences of rich white men, and sex in safe and discreet venues also generated vast sums of money. He did not doubt that some of these perversions could be used to produce favours in the future, so he was happy to incorporate them in the overall business plan. He had his own small private coven within the development and he was happy with all that.

So he had a multi layered business venture that offered legitimate golf, spa and leisure facilities, with meeting places for those for a variety of needs both business and of course pleasure.

But all this was a mere sideshow for the possible main event.

What he was really excited about was the possibility that contained somewhere within Guy's Cliff was a copy of the Agrippa. Alive but chained, waiting to be released by an Initiate such as himself.

No one had found it but from his enquiries and research,

somewhere in that building or in the grounds, was the beloved Agrippa.

A man who could control the Agrippa and work in tandem with it, not dominate or be dominated but as a beautiful and powerful partnership, would have unbelievable power, wealth and influence.

Julian Castide was no fool. He had found the Grimoires and worked their words and the practices, finding them hugely satisfactory. To say that they had worked for him, was an understatement.

In his arrogance and in his belief in himself and his skills as a modern day sorcerer being the real thing, he could understand that the Grimoires could be seen as superstitious nonsense. But the Grimoires' power lay in the fact that others believed it. A bit like faith and the existence of God or the Devil in whatever form of belief around the World. Together Julian Castide and the Grimoires had worked deliciously together.

If the Agrippa was real and it was in Guy's Cliff waiting for him then their joint power would unleash great things.

Julian Castide had risen from an unremarkable background. His parents worked in a car factory in Nantes, not Tours as he told people and had told Lucille the same. Julian was an only child. He went to school and then college and then university. His parents were proud of him because he had better himself than they had and had been awarded a scholarship to study as they could not afford to support him.

His father had had to retire early from work because of ill health and his mother was a part time secretary at the same factory. When he left home for Paris at the age of 18, he went to work in a market research company in Paris. He also studied for a degree in Psychology part time. Both his parents had died within six months of his leaving home. Julian Castide was alone in the world in terms of family.

Alone, he had simply reinvented himself with a background that was untraceable.

In terms of life he was always popular. Women loved him and physically swooned when they met him and his male friends hung around with him because he was a magnet for women. In business, he found an ease in which to operate and manipulate. He trained himself to have a more piercing gaze, his voice to become more mesmerising.

He was befriended by a couple, Louis and Helen Allende, who could see his potential immediately. They were occultists and they made no bones about it. Others would describe them as swingers but that was because they mixed with a range of people, who others defined as perverted or deviant rather than how they described themselves as open and esoteric. Julian Castide was entranced by the couple and ready made for their practices and views.

To them, their occult interests were their religion. They did not sacrifice chickens or attend orgies. They believed in the powers of potions and spells, in summoning up the supernatural.

Julian was brought into their fold not to be a third person in bed with them but as an Initiate who clearly had abilities and from there his interest grew and his practices developed. Naturally he joined them in bed sometimes, but not often.

Now at the age of 36, he was considered to have powerful magical insight and abilities and a small but influential group of men and women worshiped behind him.

His role was to assist them in trying to find what they desired, to unleash what they needed. He kept his own practices private and secret.

Julian Castide had learned much and from what he had read and studied, he understood that he had the tools to be powerful.

But Julian Castide had also grown in other ways. Gone was the happy single child with loving parents. He was becoming a monster of sorts. His power over everyone, especially women was intoxicating. Now he was in danger of becoming a monster as he found that he taking sex and control to a dangerous level of sadism. Most of the time, he was able to control it but his impending meeting with the Agrippa would, he hoped, produce yet new horizons.

He could be cruel and then charming and know how to turn this on and off and how to deflect guilt onto who he was inflicting it upon.

His drinking and cocaine use caused him to sometimes lose control and this heady mixture made him feel like a time bomb ready to explode. His obsession with the Agrippa had grown out of all proportion.

Sometimes when we look back at someone's history or back story we ask 'so what changed? What happened to make this happen? The answer in Julian Castide's case was nothing really. He was just evolving through his learning, through the people he met, through the possibilities that he saw. He started to think outside of the social norms, the possibility of wealth and power all became their own intoxicants.

He did not appear to have bad genes or a propensity for being unpleasant as a child or a teenager. Or maybe he did once he was far enough away from loving, caring parents. Who can say?

What can be said is that Julian Castide is a dangerous and vengeful man when he wants to be. Julian looked upon the development of his golf and club project next to La Croix de Bois as like planting the apple tree in Eden. It would inevitably lead to temptation and then to trouble. In his brief time around the village he already knew where and who the trouble for him was.

He had taken an instant dislike to one or two people. The Mayor for starters needed to be bought under his control. He was clearly a wily operator. He was probably a good poker player as he did not give away what he was thinking.

So far he had been helpful and courteous but at the end of the day he was a politician and by Julian Castide's code, a politician could not and never should be trusted. A belief that was shared by many if not most of the population.

Then there was that old fool. The locals called him the Professor. Now there was a man who knew far too much. He was also someone who made Julian Castide feel uncomfortable. He could not put his finger on it. He seemed to be spiritually juxtaposed to himself and that worried him. He was clearly a potential troublemaker. He would need to be put in his place but he needed to be investigated more thoroughly first.

He had also met the hopelessly attractive pharmacist and she also seemed to have a presence about her that he needed to be wary of. What was it about La Croix de Bois? It was almost as if they had a set of secret guardians in their presence! The question was why?

She also sat on the council group, which made her influential and a potential problem.

Then there was that little group of old men. The way two of them had looked at him with a mixture of amusement and disgust angered him. He did not know their names or their role in the village but he would get an investigator to find out and to have them watched.

The fact that it was Gerard, Jean Paul and myself was somewhat of a surprise.

Chapter 15 - Farid and the red monk money

Amira and Akira had settled into school. They went by coach each day to the school at a larger village. The first month had been difficult, but after that period they had integrated well with the other students in their class. Farid was astounded at how quickly they had picked up speaking French. They were way ahead of Farid, who had attended lessons but still struggled with even the basic of sentences.

But that was young people for you and their ability to adjust and learn, already leaving him behind.

Yara was at college and studying fashion design and fabrics, along with marketing. She had a job on Saturday working in a small local clothes shop and was happy. The village of La Croix de Bois was a little too quiet for her liking but she felt safe the whole time.

Jemal and Ibrahim both had part time apprenticeships combined with study, provided through the French refugee scheme, Jemal was a trainee electrician and Ibrahim a trainee eboniste (a furniture maker) as the French liked to call it.

Jemal was also playing football for the local La Croix de

Bois team and was having a trial with Dinan Lehon FC, who played in the Breton National League.

Farid dreamed of one day having a bee farm again. He had talked of his dream and had two hives in the garden of the O'Keefes, where they now lived. Jean Paul and Linda had also let him have hives in their own two gardens.

There were also to be further introductions.

Jean Paul had introduced me to Farid when they first arrived in La Croix de Bois and I found him an immensely interesting man. What he had gone through along with his family was unimaginable to me and he seemed to harbor no grudges, just a determination to look to the future and that of his children.

It was with great delight that Farid was introduced to Karen and Alain Dupont through Jean Paul and myself. When they found out what Farid had done for a living, they invited him to set up some hives on their smallholding and in return Farid was happy to work three days a week on the farm, which freed Karen up to attend two more markets to sell their products.

Ryan and Rose Marie visited after the first year and it was strange for them to see their house in reality no longer their house. It was a little unsettling though the Khalils made them welcome. However they were delighted to see them so settled.

They also told them that the house was theirs for at least another two years but Farid insisted that they could not stay there unless they took over paying for the electricity and water and the local taxes and that they repair some of the outstanding work needed on the house as well as decorating.

The Khalil's had been living in La Croix de Bois for just over a year, when the next surprise came into Farid's life. He and his family were now known in La Croix de Bois. They were known as the Syrian refugee family but that came with a certain amount of respect for Farid and his family and for the French government in giving them refugee status in France.

The O'Keefes had made that happen but the kids were all liked and Farid was always happy to help out anywhere in the village with work.

Jean Paul and Gerard had not been able to distribute all the red monk money and still had some in Jean Paul's shed, so they chatted with the Mayor and myself and we all agreed that Farid should receive 500 euros. At first he did not understand it and he had to ask Jean Paul what it was.

Of course Jean Paul spun the agreed line and who the red monks were.

This of course gave Farid great amusement and a sense of irony that 1,000 years later, he, a descendant of a Saracen, an infidel in the eye of the crusaders should not only be living in the land of the Crusaders but also be given 500 euros by a Knight Templar.

Jean Paul had not thought of this and found it equally amusing as did I when I was told.

Farid spent the entire 500 euros on wood. He wanted to fulfill a dream and to have beehives again, so he started to build them with Ibrahims help.

Ibrahim had watched Farid build the first of these hives, so when the money came from the red monks he was happy to design and build the new hives ready for the future. The two other apprentices whom he was working with, along with the qualified eboniste trainer were happy to help build new hives with him.

Chapter 16 - The Rise of the Sans Permis Car

The Mayor swung his head from side to side.

'Tomorrow is market day' he complained, 'tomorrow is sans permis day. It is the day that we are invaded by those little cars as everyone from the villages drive in to do their shopping. The place sounds like a cross between a sewing machine convention and a hornets nest.'

We laughed.

'Jean Paul may well be correct about the invasion of the Pizza but there is a far worse one - those bloody sans permis cars. The drivers are made up from three groups, those who have no licence and have never driven, not even a sit on lawnmower. Then there are the alcoholics who are banned from driving. Lastly, there are the really scary ones. The men and women who have lost their husbands and wives and have seen fit to finally drive themselves to the shop or the bar out of necessity because their old man or missus is dead and buried in the ground.'

We all laughed again.

'It's scary, that's what it is' The Mayor concluded. 'And

come market day, they seem to arrive in swarms'.

The proper term for one of these cars is a VSP - voiture sans permis. You do not need a driving licence to drive one and you can drive one from the age of 14.

'That is all legal,' the Mayor continued, '14 years old! You cannot legally smoke or drink or even get married but you can drive one of them. You can be a chronic drunk, banned from drinking and still be handed over the keys to one of those Fred Flintstone cars.'

In theory, a driver should have a little practice but in reality it never happens. The Insurers will not check and around here the Gendarmes probably will not either, especially as they usually patrol the slip roads off the motorways and the sans permis cars are banned from going on the motorway.

The reason for that is that they drive very slowly, up to about a top speed of 45 kph. You can get them supped up very simply up but illegally.

'By tightening the elastic band on them' according to Gerard.

You will definitely hear them coming before you see them and they always sound like the choke is stuck on full. The modern ones still sound odd, more like a lawn mower but modern technology has reduced the noise to more like a sewing machine.

The old ones however belch smoke, sound like they are about to break down and look like a death trap. Their speed is dedicated to creating traffic tailbacks on the country roads and the person driving this two seater usually needs a cushion to sit on in order to see over the steering wheel. They may be translated as 'the car with no licence' but it is the driver who needs no licence.

You'll probably hear them coming first, a high-pitched whine, being run at full throttle.

What I sort of admire is how they are maintained or should I say not maintained engine wise but the bodywork usually bears all the hallmarks of expert home maintenance. It is not unusual to see a bungee holding on a door handle or an old washing line tying the number plate to the body.

The paint work has often been matched with a similar colour that the rest of the tin had gone on a door or even a wall. And of course it has been brushed on with an old brush so the bristle marks are clear to see where either the metal has been too hot when the paint went on or was still wet when driven away allowing it to show some unintentional 'go faster' streaks.

In France banning someone for drunk driving effectively stops them driving a car that can do damage to everyone else as well as themselves, but it does not stop them driving and it does not stop them drinking.

However a collision in a VSP is likely to render the driver of it with a lot more damage than the person in the ordinary car and if they go into a ditch then it will probably crumple up flat, and if not can probably be dragged out of the ditch by the inebriated driver.

Like I said, the modern ones are a bit different. Bill Brown the American drives one. He has air conditioning, a reversing camera and top notch sound system. He laughs at the fact that everyone thinks he has been banned for drunk driving but the truth of the matter is that as a Californian his licence is not valid in France to drive a car other than a hired car. He is probably the only exception to the general driving population of the sans permis car in the whole of France.

.

On my walk around the market and the village the next day, I counted nine VSP's and that did not include Bill Brown's.

Chapter 17 - The Mayor explains certain things

Julian Castide had entered the Mayor's office and walked towards him and warmly shook his hand.

'Hello again Mr Mayor. Thank you for inviting me'. He took a seat at the Mayor's invitation and sat across the desk looking directly into the Mayor's eyes.

' I wanted to thank you again for organising the public meeting ten days ago. It was a very useful and important event for us. Naturally we want the whole process and development to go smoothly and with the office of the Mayor in support we are confident that this can happen'. Julian Castide said.

He never looked away from the Mayor and he never blinked. His voice was melodic and almost like a song. It was entrancing and the Mayor felt transfixed.

They sat talking for five minutes about the proposal and then Julian Castide felt in his pocket and pulled out an envelope that looked fairly thick and placed it on the desk.

'In appreciation of all your help to date, I wanted to leave this envelope with you'. He pushed the envelope gently towards the Mayor.

'Will you excuse me while I go to the toilet? When I return in a few minutes, it is my greatest wish you will have taken the envelope and placed it in the drawer of your desk. Do you agree?' He asked, snapped his fingers and rose from his chair.

The Mayor nodded and Julian stood up and left the office, closing the door behind him quietly.

The Mayor looked at the envelope and picked it up. It was open and he could see a substantial number of fifty euro notes. His hands froze in mid air and then he stopped himself and dropped the envelope back on the table breathing heavily.

Since he had become the Mayor he had always tried to do the right thing. As a younger man he had always been tempted with shortcuts and easy options, which sometimes had not resulted in the right outcome. Now as the Mayor he had responsibilities to the commune.

He had probably crossed the line over a few occurrences since being the Mayor but not for his own gain and as it turned out very much to the gain of the commune.

The envelope was sitting there in front of him and it was tempting him still and Julian Castide's warm words were flowing through his head. It would be the simplest thing in the world just to pick it up and put it in his desk drawer. No-one would be the wiser.

'Just pick it up and put it in the drawer, that's all you've got to do' he heard a voice in his head.

'Put it in the drawer and worry about it after he he has gone', came another voice.

'And anyway, he could use the money for good purposes, not for himself. That would be OK. They had done that the last time and it all turned out well', said yet another voice

'Would anyone be the wiser?' the Mayor heard Julian Castide's soft melodic voice.

'NOOOOoooo' he finally heard his own voice.

He, the Mayor would not be the wiser for taking the money. He would be the fool, who had let himself down and that was all that mattered at that moment. Julian Castide would be the wiser as he the Mayor, would be in his pocket with this envelope of money. But it changed everything. In fact it changed everything whether he took the money or refused it.

His head swam. He felt like someone who was disobeying a request or an order. It was the most peculiar feeling. That feeling was interrupted when Mr Castide re-entered the room. He walked across the room and looked at the Mayor and then at the desk and the envelope.

The Mayor stood up and looked at Julian Castide.

'It was good to meet you again Mr Castide. May I wish you well with the development of the golf course and club. I think that you have left something of your's on my desk, so please do not forget to take it with you. Good day to you' and the Mayor walked him to the door.

Julian Castide's eyes flashed anger and they darkened to almost a black colour. He said nothing. He picked up the envelope and left without a word.

The Mayor went back to his desk and slumped into his chair suddenly overwhelmed with tiredness and not a little relief. He felt he had come so close to letting himself down, so close to taking the money. It had been a monumental struggle to say 'no'.

To say 'no' even through as an older man, he knew there

would always be comebacks. The money was not a nice present, not even a thoughtful thank you. It was a bribe to shut the Mayor up, as simple as that and how dare that man even try to suggest that he was corruptible.

The man was smooth and seductive. Had he been hypnotised or did Mr Castide have terrible powers of persuasion that gnawed into you, just because you were persuadable?

The Mayor sat alone for ten minutes and then put on his jacket and walked out of his office and over to the bar where Gerard, Jean Paul and I had just met up and were sitting.

He ordered a Pastis, which was a surprise as it was only 11.00 am and we all had a coffee in front of us.

We gave him time to collect his thoughts and stop his hands from shaking. Then he related what had just happened to him.

'I may be many things but I do not take bribes' stated the Mayor.

'We know that' Gerard explained.

'That's not to say that I have not been tempted in the past. like our little settlement over the discovered money and the payment of the old people's home. That was a little close to the mark but no, never for my own back pocket'. He said

'The issue here is that I wanted to say yes because he was so scary, so corrupt. His eyes were almost black and his voice is like a low hypnotic hum. I could feel myself sinking and growing warm and drowsy and that I wanted to shout 'yes'.

'I wanted to obey his wish, to do what he was saying. He sounded so melodic and convincing'. The Mayor continued and then repeated almost trance like what Julian Castide had said to him

'Those were his exact words and they were warm and made sense to me. It was like one of those shows you see on television and the hypnotist is making you do something that you have no control over.' The Mayor continued on his confessional.

'He left the room. He left the room and there was the envelope on the desk and all I had to do was pick it up and place it in the drawer. It felt like the most natural thing to do and I was reaching for it and then I picked it up and then suddenly I heard another voice and then another voice and another. I cannot say who it was but it was like a cold bucket of water being thrown over me. My hand immediately let go of the envelope and it fell back onto my desk. It was as if the envelope was trying to poison me.'

'When he returned I was sitting on my chair and looked at him calmly and wished him well with the development and that he had left something on the desk that was his. Then his lip curled up at the end of his mouth. His eyes seemed even blacker then before. He picked up his envelope and departed. Then I was trembling. I was so proud of myself that I had said no or something had helped me say no but I also felt a fear deep in my heart, a deep seated dread.'

'So you see, I am not some wonderfully strong and honest person. I was so close to taking the money it scared me' and with that the Mayor sat back.

'Well done' Gerard said

'Bravo' Jean Paul followed up.

'Don't beat yourself up. The thing is you did not take the money. You did not succumb to the temptation, the hypnosis. Take the credit for what you did, or should I say what you didn't do' I said, by way of encouragement and as honesty as I saw it.

'Thank you for your kind words' the Mayor said.

'So what do we do? The man is clearly dangerous and what he wants to do with Guys' Cliff and the extremes he is prepared to go to does not bode well' Gerard asked.

Chapter 18 - Bees

'Albert Einstein stated that if the bee disappears from the surface of the Earth, man would have no more than four years left to live.' Jean Paul announced to us all.

'Did he really say that? Arthur Barnes asked.

' Apparently' Jean Paul said.

' I would imagine it is a quote greatly used by every Greenpeace person in the world' Gerard stated.

'And beekeepers' Arthur chipped in.

'Seriously, if that were to happen then we would lose all the plants that the bees pollinate. Then what would happen, every animal that eats plants would die because there were no plants and then the meat eaters would die out because their prey was not alive and onwards and upwards to us.'

'And in that process of decline there would not be enough food for everyone, the supermarkets would go short and there would be social chaos and collapse.'

We all looked at Jean Paul.

'You are turning into a right doom monger Jean Paul,' Arthur suggested.

'But it's true isn't it' his wife Janine said. 'I don't know about bees but the facts seem to bear out the troubles we are all having with global warming and pesticides and rising sea levels. Even here, we are having hotter and drier summers and then when it rains a month's worth seems to come down in a day and we all get flooded because it cannot run off fast enough'.

Perhaps we are lucky here and do not see it because we still have woodlands and orchards for the cider apples and other fruits, we have fields where they rotate the crops and plant wild flowers so the bees are around and survive here.

'And we all have gardens where we grow a load of flowers,' Arthur agreed.

'That's right,' Jean Paul agreed, the honey bee can thrive in gardens, woodlands, orchards, meadows and other areas where flowering plants are abundant. They build their nests where they are safe from predators inside the cavity of trees or under things like the guttering of houses. The trouble seems to be all the pesticides and chemicals that farming and gardeners use all the time to kill bugs and things.'

'Well thank you Jean Paul' Gerard raised his glass, 'very educational. Where did you learn all this about bees?'

'From Farid of course. He tends to the two bee hives in my garden. He used to be a bee farmer in Syria with over 100 hives to manage until the war destroyed their town and his farm'.

It was another conversation that we would all return to shortly and in the context of our own local environment.

Chapter 19 - The Dead

While we pondered who the man Julian Castide was, we had to try and understand the threat that he was presenting. We were coming to understand what the professor had told us about Guy's Cliff and the dark history within it. Now we could clearly understand what the Mayor had just experienced.

Were we just becoming the latest contributors to a long line of intrigue about the place? My own experiences of, to put it simply, the 'unknown', of life and death, good and evil, right and wrong, believing what we see and hear are interesting.

I have always been able to see the dead. They are never ghostly apparitions or scary flashes or shadows like you watch on TV, on some of those ghost programmes. Neither are they spirits that communicate with me like they do with clairvoyants. For me, It is like watching glimpses of a film, almost like out takes but with a sense of realism.

They just seem to be going about their daily business, as if they are still living. Perhaps they are and I am seeing history like some fold in space and time. I only see them in certain places but all of them in La Croix de Bois. I never saw these people or ghosts until I came to the village. It does not happen everyday but it is fairly regular.

It has never been a thing to be fearful of. To me, it is just a natural and normal thing. I talk about it very little as it unsettles people and they think that I am odd or mad.

I do not think of them as ghostly apparitions from the past haunted and unable to leave their earthly realm. They do not appear as roaming tormented spirits. They seem like men and women in their own time, living a moment in their own lives, going about their daily business oblivious to me or any of us.

I guess that I have also found a natural habitat to see them living in Brittany

In Brittany there is a huge vein of tales of ghosts and ghostly apparitions. That is and always has been its folklore.

There is a commonly held Breton tradition, that there is no significant separation between the living and the dead. The living and the dead dwell in two discrete worlds. These worlds overlap in perpetual relation with one another.

That thin line between the two can be seen if you choose

to look and tradition has it that there are special days when the veil is dropped, namely on All Souls Day, Christmas Eve and Midsummer's Eve

A very old tradition is that on the evening of All Souls Day, the dining or kitchen table is covered in a white cloth and food is laid out for the dead. Many would then depart to bed so as to avoid seeing the dead or give them some peace but I prefer to sit and drink with them into the early hours, sharing stories and laughter.

With early religion, the dead and departed were revered and the desire to see them and visit them was part of those beliefs but with Christianity for various reasons, people started to fear the dead. I am of the opposite opinion. I am as happy listening to the birds singing in the day as I am the dead rustling leaves on the bushes outside my door.

Across Brittany there are differing times attributed to when any of us might see the dead. Along the coast it was between midnight and the dawn and in central Brittany between ten and two. Of course around the area of the east of Brittany where La Croix de Bois is, then the ghostly apparitions seem to like anytime on a Tuesday evening for some reason.

Why a Tuesday? Who can say how that little idea has

evolved or twisted into the tale that it now is. A bit like the washerwomen at night can only be seen by men who are intoxicated on their way home from the bar that I have told you about previously. These old tales need to be listened to in the context of their history and who is telling it.

North of La Croix de Bois are the villages, where white faced and white cloaked priests are sometimes seen at night.

South of La Croix de Bois, these white faced apparitions are only seen by women. Unmarried women at that.

There is a Château La Hunaudaye, not too far from Lamballe that has someone called the blower (le souffle in french) who walks around its ramparts and in the woods that surround the castle is a red robbed man, who seeks retribution from a former lord of the castle, who murdered his family. I have seen neither of these souls but would be happy to try and help alleviate their torment if I could find the means.

Perhaps it is all in my head and my strong sense of history and desire to try and see the history of somewhere, makes me see things that do not really exist apart from inside my head.

As I said I choose not to talk to everyone around the village because unless they can see for themselves then they are sceptical or a little perturbed, or in Jean Paul's case I would be at the mercy of his endless banter and piss taking.

But I have listened to Jean Paul talk about his childhood and the grand parents, who would cover the mirrors with bed sheets when a storm was coming so as not to see the reflection of the devil in the lightning; the hell and damnation that would befall you if you sinned, the risks to your soul of false fornication. I think that Jean Paul is a reasonably normal guy but growing up with that has taken a long time for him to throw off those shackles of belief off.

Jean Paul deals with many things with humour and laughter and needs no further excuses to take the piss out of me or anyone for that matter, not even Linda, his close female friend, who as I look at the height of the sun in the sky is probably still in bed asleep as it must be between 10.00 and 11.00 in the morning.

It is a beautiful morning and Linda is missing it and the evil that surrounds Guys Cliff and Julian Castide seems far away but I have a feeling that it is seeping into our village, and fast.

Chapter 20 - The business case

The final Environmental Impact Plan found an overwhelming case in support of the Golf Course proposal.

Julian Castide had worked wonders on the environmental impact assessment team. They along with men and women who sat on the appropriate boards at the cotes d'Armor department level and the regional level had not been as resistant as the Mayor and even better, not particularly hard on what they needed in their expense accounts.

The development was thought to be excellent. It was going to be a model green development that did not use pesticides or hormones, and would improve the local habitat in terms of flora and fauna.

So instead of a zero impact on the environment it was actually going to have a positive impact, so the report claimed, which seemed fairly remarkable as it would involve new roads and bulldozers and so forth.

The construction would involve 50% of the local builders for labour. It would create around 7 to 10 permanent jobs and at peak times around 30 part time jobs. The whole area would get better signage and services.

It was estimated in a cost benefit analysis that local businesses would see around an additional 15% in revenue and the commune would benefit greatly from the Taxe Fonciere on the property, which meant improved services for those in need in the commune if the money was spent wisely by the Mayor and not squandered on unnecessary priorities, to which the report did not detail.

It also noted that it would give the area an elevated profile which would be good for business and tourism and kick start what was a stagnant local economy.
We read the report.

'No mention of 1,000 members of the golf club paying 3,000 euros a year for membership. That's three million to start with before anyone has even passed wind' Jean Paul stated.

'And no mention of what a private members club with hotel rooms and meeting and catering facilities is going to entail' I had said.

Gerard looked up at him after reading the report. In the USA and elsewhere, golf courses have become the new casinos for laundering and cleaning money for crime gangs. It is my guess having seen that Castide fellow and how he describes his investors that this is what he is planning here'

'You think?' Jean Paul asked.

'There is no way of proving it but that would be my guess'. He concluded, 'but that Julian Castide, he is at another level. From what the Mayor has told us and the belief that the Professor has about Guy's Cliff, then he is into something else completely on top of involving mobsters and that is scary'.

On top of the Environmental Impact Assessment Report, the article written by Lucille appeared in Quest France the very same day.

It was highly positive for the development, with the title

Brittany to get a new high quality eco golf course

It had been a very strange three days following Lucille's Interview with Julian Castide. She had gone to bed that evening exhausted but could not sleep and she had got up early the next morning and worked her way through three black coffees but her head was muddled and confused. She tried to sit at her laptop and write but her mind felt numb.

It felt like she had a hangover and knew that was not possible and in some ways she wished it had been the alcohol. She had never been so carefree and brazen sexually in her life like she had been yesterday.

For a moment she wondered whether Julian drugged her but she knew this was not true. No, she had entered into what she did willingly but like she was under some hypnosis type experience. The afternoon now had a dream-like quality to it. Almost as if it was one of those dreams that you woke from convinced that it was real.

She closed her lap top and looked out of the window.

Lucille knew what she had to do first and texted her boyfriend to see whether he was free to meet up later that day, which he was.

When they met up, she told him that she felt that they should no longer be together as a couple, that it was not really working and had lost its sparkle. She did not tell him about her encounter with Julian Castide.

To her utter shock, he agreed, he knew that she no longer felt the same about him and he about her. He was not dramatic and accepted that they had been going through the motions and was surprised that neither of them had met anyone else. He agreed that their conversation was long overdue and he apologised that he had not said anything earlier.

There was a little tear in each other's eyes and to stop it getting emotional, he gave her a hug and wished her well and left.

Lucille drove back to her flat in another mix of shock and some sadness but also as if a weight had been lifted from her. Her secret from yesterday had not been divulged and what it had triggered was to release her and him from a failing relationship

She returned home and banged out an article. Every so often she thought about herself lying naked with Julian Castide only yesterday and what an amazing man he seemed to be.

She tried to concentrate on the article, that on balance the golf course development seemed to be a wholly positive thing that it was bringing work and profile to the area and was attempting to use modern cutting edge technology as a green development.

Which of course even she knew was nonsense as the deserted land there already was green and anyone driving cars to the venue and delivering goods to the site, building the site and so forth was adding a carbon footprint.

She wrote a brief synopsis about the man behind the development - Julian Castide, that he was an intelligent and charismatic man, passionate about creating a good environment and how important it was to be in tune with nature.

As she wrote she had a nagging feeling that something was not right. How could one man be so wealthy and good looking, attentive and respectful to her and a consummate lover? In her experience, men did not come in such perfect packaging.

Yet, he had been correct about her relationship with her boyfriend. He had been a wonderful man to interview, courteous and generous, unlike many people she had had to interview and because of him she felt her life had been awakened and renewed, so writing anything negative seemed wholly wrong.

When she had sent off the article to her editor, she stood up and smiled to herself.

'Keep the experience and memory for what it was - wonderful and releasing as it turned out. You've sent in the article and get on with your life' She said to herself.

Chapter 21 – a series of mishaps

We only heard the news the following morning. The Professor had been in an accident. He was in hospital after being hit by a car. He had a broken pelvis and and a broken ankle but was alive and stable.

We went to visit him that afternoon, the three of us -Gerard, Jean Paul and myself.

The Professor was propped up in bed looking pale and probably exactly like he should look after such an accident.

We pulled up three chairs and sat down around him.

'What happened' Gerard asked.

'I was taking my daily constitutional walk. I took the road that leads up to the woods behind the village and suddenly out of nowhere a car came screeching up the hill behind me. I automatically stood back onto the grass verge and went to raise my walking stick to acknowledge them and instead he veered over and ran into me.' The professor explained.

'So do you think it was an accident from a bad bit of

driving?' Gerard followed up.

'No, he steered towards me. I saw his face and I saw him turn the wheel towards me. I tried to step out of the way hence the car only gave me a glancing blow and I fell into the shallow ditch at the side.'

'What happened then?' Gerard asked, 'did he stop or get out?'

'He slowed down after he hit me, then changed gear and drove off picking up speed as he did so. There was no one else around, no other car. The road was empty except for him and me', the Professor finished.

'Have you told this to the Gendarmes?' Gerard asked further.

'Only the fact that the driver did not stop and no I did not get the number plate, so there is little for them to go on.'

'So it was either someone who is a very bad driver and panicked and drove off or it was a hit and run?' Jean Paul summed up.

What the Professor said next chilled us all.

'We all know who was behind this – not the driver, because I did not recognise him but who ordered it – Julian Castide. I am in no doubt. Two days ago, a dead cat was left at my back door. I wondered but even then I had my suspicions. I have had a number of phone calls where there has been silence on the line. Wrong numbers? Who can say?'

The Professor sat there looking at each of us.

'Yes, before you ask, I am 100% certain that this was no accident. Now you also need to go to see how Cristal Lamarr is. Her pharmacy was broken into this morning. I heard it from one of the nurses who knows her and knows that I live in La Croix de Bois.'

We sat there reeling from both incidents.

'Don't worry about me boys' he said, 'I am bruised and battered but I'm OK. I am however a captive audience for a few weeks and going nowhere. Nowhere, just as the Guys Cliff development gets underway.'

We left and drove straight back to La Croix de Bois. Gerard rang Cristal to ask how she was and that we were coming over.

When we arrived, Cristal was sweeping the floor. She had

closed the Pharmacy for the day and sent the staff home.

Across the back wall the word 'witch' had been spray painted on it and boxes of medicines lay across the floor.

'I came into this mess when I opened up this morning. The gendarmes came and asked if anything had been stolen and what to look out for but the curious thing is that nothing seems to have been stolen. It is too early to be definitive about that, but I can see nothing obvious has been taken.'

'Are you OK?' Jean Paul asked.

'No I'm angry. Angry about that' and she pointed to the word 'witch' in bright red paint across the wall.

'The gendarmes said it was probably kids but of course it isn't it. It's a message about me. A warning to me.'

'About your abilities?' I said.

'Yes of course,' Cristal answered.

Jean Paul was doing what he did best and was clearing up the boxes. Gerard looked at me and Cristal.

'You are a natural Healer and a Pharmacist', Gerard stated

'Gerard, we have all known one another a long time and you know my abilities are slightly more than those. I could never explain it myself only that I inherited it from my mother and she from my grand mother but we never advertised that fact, never talked about it but you three know or suspect and certainly the Professor knows because he seems to know everything about all of us. I also sit on the committee and work closely with the Mayor.'

'Meaning?' Gerard asked.

'Meaning, I am being advertised as a witch, the Mayor is scared shitless after they tried to bribe him and the poor old Professor is in hospital after someone tried to run him over. This has all happened after the Guys' Cliff proposal. What else to say? This is a warning to me to shut the fuck up. It could not be clearer', the beautiful but angry Pharmacist and Healer concluded.

'What can we do?' Jean Paul asked.

'I don't know if we can do anything to be honest but I think the three of you need to get into Guys' Cliff and try and see if you can find anything'.

Chapter 22 - A terrifying Search

So it was decided. We needed to go and try and find out for ourselves

We knew that there would be security on or around the site. We decided to go at twilight, which visually is an uneasy time when the light can play tricks but we knew that we could not bumble around in the dark. The place may well be haunted by centuries of terrible happenings In addition there may well be a terrifying book, that could come alive on the premises. Jean Paul had not steadied our nerves by suggesting such a book, if it did exist was probably protected by unimaginable creatures.

We reminded him that this was not some paranormal type lock down programme on TV. Our plan was to disturb no one, neither security guards nor demons. We were going at twilight because we could not walk around shining torches and anyway, we did not have night vision goggles.

Though it was a great surprise that Jean Paul never conjured a pair up from somewhere in his house, he seemed to have everything else there was, acquired from some market or house clearance he had attended. His ability to find and I guess look for things that are never on the radar of the rest of us was formidable. But now this time we were going in literally with only our eyes open.

We crept through the trees and undergrowth watching for anyone on guard duty. Just outside a side door, Jean Paul tripped on something on the ground. We all froze as he looked down.

'Mother of God' he exclaimed and we all looked at what was by his feet. It was a very large dog bowl.

'What type of hound drinks out of such a large bowl? Look at the bloody size of that' He continued. Gerard and I looked at it and agreed that it was indeed a very large bowl.

'So we know the security people here have a guard dog,' Gerard concluded, 'best plan then is for you to always lead the way Jean Paul'.

We entered the building through the side door where the dog bowl was . We crept as quietly as possible into what seemed like an old washroom and along a corridor that took us to a large room, which had further rooms off to the left and right of it. Devoid of furniture and curtains it all had a sparse but looming presence.

In the dying sunlight, the rooms seemed huge. We walked on and into yet another large room and from there we could see what was the kitchen.

As we approached the kitchen, the sense of foreboding increased in me and I looked at Gerard and Jean Paul and I could see that they were anxious as well. Jean Paul had a slight tremor. Into the kitchen, which contained a very old sink and work surface but nothing else. All of a sudden all three of us felt gripped by an intense feeling of unease. It was hard to describe, almost like the shock you get from static electricity but none of us were touching anything.

My head started to throb and Gerard turned to me.

'My head is beginning to hurt. It feels like I have had a sudden headache.'

'Do you feel the cold in this room?' Jean Paul asked, and indeed I could. We were all feeling the same thing. Running off from the kitchen were a number of doors. One was open and led to what was probably a pantry or storage room but the next two doors were shut.

Gerard went to open the first closed door by placing his hand on the door knob and immediately let go and muttered something that was inaudible to Jean Paul and I.

The door was jammed shut and the handle hard to turn.

'I have to get out,' he said finally, 'my head is banging'.

'Agreed' Jean Paul said immediately and turned around and walked out. I stood there looking at the closed door until I realised that I was now alone in the kitchen and followed them out and stopped them.

'Listen guys we have come this far, we can't just leave now' I said. We were just five metres from the kitchen door, when suddenly we heard a sort of bang. It sounded like something slipping or falling as the noise sort of developed and ended in a bang.

We all looked at each other. That was it. We all started to run back through the larger rooms and to the side door that we had come through. We spilled out into the open air. It was now definitely dusk, the sun was below the horizon and the air was hazy. I would describe it as a mist but tried to dismiss this as imagining it because of where we were.

What we saw instead was torch beams, two of them shining right at us.

'Stop' came a shout.

We did not obey, we just ran. We ran with no concern that they might be armed or we should stop and try and explain to the guards that we were just curious locals. No chance, we ran for the trees and the road where we had left the car further down. We ran for at least half a kilometre, until we came out onto the road, where we stopped breathless.

'That was intense,' Gerard said.

'Intense? It was fucking scary that what it was' Jean Paul said. I nodded in agreement but remained silent trying to process what I had just felt.

'It hasn't changed one bit. I ran out tonight like I ran out when I was a kid. That was like groundhog day.' Jean Paul confessed still breathing heavily with his hands on his hips catching his breath.

'At least you didn't shit yourself this time' Gerard laughed and then walked behind Jean Paul, 'oh no' he said peering at Jean Paul's derriere, 'maybe you have'.

'How can you make a joke like that at this moment in time? There's something wrong with you' he said to Gerard.

We walked to the car and got in and Gerard started up the engine.

'There is definitely something wrong with that place' Jean Paul said as we headed back to the village.

'Do you think that they recognised us?' I said.

'Of course they did, we were not exactly covered up and how many old duffers like us hang around together in La Croix de Bois? We will be getting a visit from someone. There's no debate about that and hopefully after what happened to the poor old Professor and Cristal, lets hope its the gendarmes and no one else'. Gerard concluded.

'Who in their right mind would want to be a security guard walking around that place? Someone from casting for the living dead, if you ask me' Jean Paul concluded and I would not argue with that assessment.

But what to do?

We went straight to the bar and ordered Ricard with very little water. We thought about telephoning the hospital to see if we could speak with the Professor but we thought better of it. Did they really need to know that we had broken into Guys Cliff and found nothing nor seen anything but that without sounding overly dramatic, the place felt evil and played with our minds.

We had all tried and come up short.

As things stood, we had a planning proposal that looked on paper that it would bring jobs and money to the area, there was an Environmental Impact Assessment that again on paper ticked all the boxes, an extremely engaging and charismatic front man in Julian Castide, heading a wealthy consortium, who were winning the public relations battle hands down outside of La Croix de Bois.

From our point of view, we knew that the development of Guys' Cliff was much more than a new golf club and hotel. It came with private members and business meeting facilities. Julian Castide was not only corrupt and powerful but dangerous and had intentions that went way beyond this golf course development. He wanted it because he knew that something evil lurked in the building.

I had told Jean Paul and Gerard that according to the Professor that evil was a book called an Agrippa that might be present somewhere in the house that was capable of controlling minds and even the weather. We had agreed to tell no one else.

After this evening, I knew what the Professor had told me was true. It was without a shadow of doubt locked behind one of those doors off the kitchen. I could sense it and I knew that Jean Paul and Gerard had felt it too.

'I rather fear that if that thing is unlocked especially by that Castide chap, then we are in deep, deep trouble and I fear for the commune of La Croix de Bois' I said and with that Jean Paul ordered more drink.

But worse was to come, as Jean Paul walked out with three more glasses of Pastis, a gendarme car pulled to a halt and the two officers climbed out. Gerard recognised one of them.

'Gentlemen, I am afraid that I have had a report that three men illegally broke into Guys Cliff this evening. The description the security guards gave us fits the three of you perfectly'.

Quick as a flash Jean Paul asked, 'when was this supposed to happen and what was the description of these so called trespassers?'

'You don't want to ask about how they described you' the Gendarme said smiling, 'its not very flattering and they even suggested that we would probably find you in the bar here'.

'What? Are they psychic as well as observant' Jean Paul mused and poured the pastis down his throat.

You will have to accompany us to the Gendarmerie for questioning over the offence.

Whichever way you looked at it we had failed and we were fresh out of ideas. In addition, we were now being arrested for trespass, or even worse, breaking and entering.

Chapter 23 - Julian Castide

Julian Castide himself had been utterly shocked that the Mayor had refused to take the money that he had offered him. It had been a sizable sum of money, along with promises of future involvement in the project.

Julian Castide was not used to such a rebuff. The power of his mind had grown and grown and he considered it more formidable now than it had ever been and this weak minded old fool of a Mayor had turned him down.

The effect of this refusal was disturbing. If this could happen with all the power that he had learned to use, then he needed to develop further. Clearly Julian Castide needed to be with the Agrippa. Julian Castide needed to find the Agrippa sooner rather than later. Not sooner but now.

The morning after our arrest, he had been informed of the news about the arrest of the three men lurking around Guys' Cliff. He knew the Professor was in hospital and that the old bastard was out of commission for a few weeks and he was very happy with the warning that had been delivered to the Pharmacist.

Now he could turn his attentions to finding the Agrippa before the builders moved in to commence work on the refurbishment.

He had set off the next day and headed to Guys' Cliff. If this Grimoire known as the Agrippa was there then it would guide him to it. When he parked up just behind the building, he took a long line of cocaine. He felt that the cocaine would sharpen and heighten his perceptions and he entered the building.

He had walked through the buildings looking again into all the rooms and then into the kitchen. In the kitchen his head immediately tightened. He looked around the kitchen. There were three doors in addition to the one that he had come in from.

The first led to a storage room, with the shelves still standing in them. The second door was locked and he went to the third and although a little jammed, he managed to shove it open. Inside it was empty, probably where the freezers and fridges had been kept.

He returned to the locked door and stood back and looked at it. Then he went up close to it and rested his head against the door. A sharp pain shot through his temple. He could sense something behind the door. But the door was shut tight.

He shoved against it and it moved slightly. He searched the walls to see whether there was a key hanging anywhere but to no avail. He kicked the door and it moved in its frame but did not open.

He searched around for something to jam in between the door and its frame. He walked back out into the other rooms and finally by a fireplace he found an old iron used for poking the wood in the fire. He almost ran back to the kitchen and thrust the poker into the gap and started to try and prise it open.

The door gave way slightly and he reinserted the poker and pushed against the door as he did so. Then he stopped and kicked the door in frustration. Julian Castide was sweating and he thrust the poker again into the gap between frame and door and shoved with all the power that he could.

He thought that the poker which was rusted was going to bend and then all of a sudden the door moved. He had not pushed the lock out of the door frame but it had moved.

He tried again and this time the latch gave away and he threw the door wide open and lurched into the room behind it.

The room was about six metres by four metres. There was a small window at head height to one side. The window overlooked the river and the outside drop was considerably higher than that inside the room. The only other thing in the room was an old armoire.

He went up to the armoire and touched it. What seemed like an electric current shot threw him and he let go. His head was throbbing. He pulled open the door of the cupboard and saw that inside it was empty. He stood back and looked at the armoire and then grabbed it, ignoring the feeling that was pulsing through him and started to shove the armoire and then went to the side of it and pushed it.

With all his strength he pushed it at the side but it still would not move. He picked up the poker and in a frenzy started to smash the poker into the wood. It started to splinter and then he tore at the door frame and it began to loosen. He went back to pushing the side of the piece of the furniture and tried to wedge the poker under the two of the legs.

After much frantic straining he managed to lift the two legs off the ground up. He kicked the pieces of wood that had splintered under the two legs, used them as a kind of pivot and finally it was on one side of its legs. With one final shove to it tilted over and smashed to the ground. He pushed the armoire to one side. These old pieces of furniture were so well built that it remained full intact as it lay on its side.

What it had been covering was a small wooden set of shutters about one and a half metres from the floor. The shutters were like the one's on the outside of the windows in French houses.

The pain in his head sharpened and he knew he had found Agrippa. They had found one another. He picked up the poker and returned to the shutters. He started to thrust the poker at the very old shutters that were sealed tight and rusted. There was a chain threaded through it and he tried to place the poker between the chain and the shutters.

It would not budge, so he took the poker and started to smash it into the wood and try to splinter it. Over the next five minutes any observer would have described Julian Caside as looking like the devil possessed and indeed perhaps this would have been an accurate description.

Finally, the shutters gave way and he pulled the remaining wood away. His heart was thumping and inside this tiny wall cavity was a sack with something inside it.

He pulled the sack out and then carefully put his hand inside the sack and felt a book. Trembling, he removed it from the sack and threw it back to the floor.

He looked at the book and stroked the cover and opened it in the middle and looked at the blank page.

'I have it' he whispered, 'I have found you' he yelled.

Chapter 24 - The Flight

Airman Thierry Lloris went through the systems checks and released the brake and his Mirage 2000 fighter jet screamed across the tarmac and into the sky. He was flying alongside another jet with Captain Henri Lavalle also in a Mirage 2000.

Their flight path would take them from their airbase at Landivisiau, near Brest and across Brittany before turning north before Dinan for the coast and back along the north Brittany coastline.

Airman Thierry Lloris loved the low level 300 metres flying. It was exhilarating and was everything that he had dreamed that it would be. He had trained for these moments for years. Privately, he was also happy to have never been involved in combat if the truth be told.

The two airmen kept close contact and the land below flashed past, towns and villages and endless fields. Halfway into their flight, Thierry's dashboard console in front of him suddenly lit up, quickly followed by the right engine stalling. He immediately tried to restart the engine without success and to his utter horror the left side engine also started to splutter.

Thierry struggled with the controls and immediately heard from his captain asking him what was happening. He knew from all his training that he had seconds to try and correct the problem and to try to hold the plane in a glide position before it started to spin.

No luck. He looked ahead and could see below but ahead of him, farmhouses and small hamlets. Then he could see a valley with a sizeable village in it. He had to eject but he had to try and clear the village before he did but he had lost all control of the plane.

Just before he pressed the ejector button, he felt what seemed like a gust of wind that veered the Mirage a little to the north. The ejector seat fired him out of the plane and into the air and then the parachute opened and he started to descend and to unscramble his brain.

Although to Airman Thierry Lloris it seems to be in slow motion he watched in seconds as the Mirage bore down to the ground at between 300 and 400 kilometres an hour and started to spin. The village lay to the south and he realised what a miracle that a gust of wind had caught the plane.

Instead it hurtled into what looked like a derelict building standing on top of a cliff and exploded into a ball of flame.

Airman Thierry Lloris barely had time to adjust his parachute as they had been flying at such a low altitude and he landed serenely in the village square.

Chapter 25 - The accident

Julian Castide could not believe his good fortune. He had the Grimoire that was called the Agrippa in his arms. He was trembling with excitement and anticipation.

For months he had wondered whether this copy existed. The rumours had been true and he should have believed in himself, instead of only wondering. He was Julian Castide, a successful businessman, an occultist with great talents, he had grown powerful, he could control people, he was handsome and now with the Agrippa that power and influence would grow.

'I have it' he whispered, 'I have found you' he yelled but was drowned out by a terrible scream from outside the window. It snatched away his attention and he looked out of the window.

The scream was a jet fighter flying right towards him. It was coming right at him and the Agrippa he held lovingly to his chest, his arms wrapped tightly around its cover. He did not have time to think nor scream. He simply evaporated as did the book known as the Agrippa on impact in the explosion.

In that moment the fledgling relationship between Julian

Castide and Agrippa vanished and was destroyed forever in an inferno of fire that the jet fighter created when it smashed into the side of the cliff and blew away the entirety of Guys' Cliff and all that was hidden away in it. No one would know they had been together or how close to catastrophe we had all come.

Ironically, legend has it that only fire could destroy the Agrippa and it had, an intense fire had burnt every last page and Julian Castide along with it.

Chapter 26 - The accident from the village

Just before Julian Castide and the book of the Agrippa were locked in an embrace and vapourised in an instant, there was a strange set of circumstances in the village of La Croix de Bois.

It was a lovely sunny day and then suddenly it had turned chilly and dull as the sun went behind the only cloud in the sky. The heat literally went out of the day and a couple of people outdoors, shuddered like you do when you feel a chill.

Maria had dropped a teapot in the bar and it had exploded across the floor.

The usual queue outside the boulangerie all stopped talking at the same time and looked up at the sky even though at that moment they could not hear nor see anything unusual.

Arthur Barnes was reversing his car out of his drive and onto the road and drove straight into the left hand pillar of his gates. Jean Paul had entered the bar but was at a complete loss as to what to order.

A number of us in the village had heard, then seen, the jet suddenly come into view with its sputtering engine, heading towards us and then it veered away, almost like it was nudged, the pilot had ejected and the plane went below our line of sight and smashed into the ground, somewhere to the north of us but not far away. We heard the explosion and then saw the rising ball of flame and smoke.

We watched the airman float harmlessly down under his parachute and landed right in front of us.

Now there is one little thing to say that when I say a number of us saw and heard the plane coming down and the subsequent explosion, not all of us did.

Linda had slept through it all. The awful noise of the jet, the explosion, the Pompier's sirens, the commotion in the village. Why that should have been a surprise to anyone as the accident was only at 10.45 in the morning, is a mystery. When she was up and about she could not understand the pandemonium that was going on and it took at least three people to convince her that the story as it was unfolding was true.

Chapter 27 - Who can say?

As I sit here telling you this, I have to admit that we had seemingly run out of options on how to stop the development. Whatever we felt and the arguments that we put forward the reports of the environmental impact assessment and the investors relationship with men in authority and decision makers further up than La Croix de Bois were saying yes and yes please.

We had resorted to cheap shots about the private members club and facilities and they had either fallen on deaf ears or been quietly welcomed by men who saw such facilities nearer to home than having to travel to Paris for their desires and perversions.

Worst of all was the potential unleashing of the Agrippa and all that might bring. The evil and control that it would assert on all of us. Was it even true? We were three simple men but even we had been shocked and we admit it, scared by what we felt that evening up in Guy's Cliff but it would have all been in our imagination put there by the Professor.

Jean Paul, Gerard and myself had pondered together privately but we did believe the Professor. We had had time to consider whether this threat was real or imagined or just the fantasy of an aged man we called the Professor, whilst we sat in the cells at the Gendarmerie. We were released the next morning and told to report back in three days.

His knowledge was steeped in the history of Brittany and all the facts and superstitions that came with it. Superstitions that had survived fifteen hundred years of Catholicism, the Inquisition and over the last hundred years modern science and technology.

Such thoughts and considerations would feed many an evening of drinks. However what we felt and heard in that dreadful place left us with very little doubt that we had all experienced something that was very unpleasant.

This is the here and now.

As we understand it, Agrippa is no more and there is a high likelihood that Julian Castide was at Guys' Cliff at the time of the explosion but there is no definitive evidence that he was there.

The impact of the jet fighter and the following explosion obliterated Guys Cliff and took some of the cliff with it into the river. The fire raged for half a day until the Pompiers could extinguish it, preferring to stop it spreading onto the land rather than saving the building.

What no-one knew was that in 1956, Tomas De Vere knew that he did not have the power to destroy the Agrippa. So he had locked a chain around a sack in which he had placed the Agrippa and shut and locked the shutters to a small cellar off of the kitchen. He had then bricked it up and placed an armoire in front of the brick work. Whether it was just bad luck or bad people or the Agrippa itself Tomas was determined that no one else would fool with it.

Somehow Julian Castide had discovered this story in his conversations and researches, through reading the Grimoires and his occultist friends, and a mix of good old fashioned gossip and hearsay. It was what fundamentally had attracted him to Guys' Cliff in the first place, although the eye watering amounts of money that could be earned from investing other people's money were also massive factor also.

Faced with an extensive renovation plan for the entire building as part of a golfing complex, the Agrippa was waiting patiently to be rediscovered. Julian Castide believed it and the Professor feared it. The rest of us were in blissful ignorance of it.

Airman Thierry Lloris's Mirage 2000 smashed into the centre of Guys Cliff and the following fireball engulfed and incinerated everything in the building. Folklore and Occultists would claim that the only way to destroy an Agrippa was through fire and this the plane had done.

When I spoke to the Professor again after the accident, he simply smiled and gave a Gallic shrug as if to indicate that it was perfectly normal and understandable.

There was also one other side to this story. When the Pompiers had declared the site safe, the forensic team had gone over the wreckage of the fighter jet in search of what had gone wrong causing it to crash.

Most of the fighter jet was embedded in the ground and rubble of the building and had been scattered over several hundred metres. Then the searing temperatures had melted most of the body of the plane. They discovered in all of this the remains of part of a motorcar engine, which they gave to the local gendarmes.

It had been assumed at the time of the crash that Guys Cliff was empty. There was no scheduled work due there and no one was there for any inspections. Security was on the perimeter and as it happens the security man on duty had been told to go home that day as he was not needed.

No one had been reported missing either.

However, it fell on Inspector Didier Lauren to instigate a search of the remains of the rubble to look in case there had been anyone there.

A team of three spent a day there but could find nothing, no bones, no personal effects, nothing, so the search ended there and then.

However the Inspector and the insurance agent then had to contact the owners of Guys' Cliff and two things became clear. Firstly, from the insurance brokers, the Inspector discovered that Guys' Cliff was still in ownership of the previous bankrupt hotel chain, as there had been a civil court case trying to establish ownership that had never been resolved.

The sale was dependent on two things, firstly the planning consent being awarded and secondly an official signing and releasing documents that were forged alleging ownership of the building to a non-existent business instead of what could be considered the rightful inheritors.

In truth, the bankrupt hotel should be transferred to its biggest creditor. That creditor was none other than the commune of La Croix de Bois.

Secondly, the Inspector discovered that Julian Castide had disappeared and no one could find him. No one at his work, or his neighbours, none of his consortium partners has seen nor heard from him since the plane crash. He is still listed as a missing person to this day.

Chapter 28 -Two Years On

Six months after the accident, the 81 hectares of Guys' Cliff, passed legally to the commune of La Croix de Bois and it became an '*experimental rewilding experimental biofarm*'. What does that mean, I hear you ask?

A chance conversation between some of the younger villagers, had reminded Jean Paul and myself about a French couple who were trying to establish a biofarm ten kilometres away and we all went to see the Mayor.

The French couple, Karen and Alain Dupont, were the couple that we had had a picnic with a few months ago, who had talked to us about the changes in Breton farming over the last fifty years.

They had visited a farm called the Knepp estate farm in Sussex near the town of Horsham a few years earlier after reading a book called 'Grazing Ecology and Forest History' by a Dutch ecologist Dr Frans Vera. It was a book that convinced them of what they wanted to do.

After visiting the people at Knepp estate they were convinced that this was what they needed to try to do in Brittany but did not have sufficient land.

In a nutshell, they wanted to introduce herbivores into a woodland setting, which would have an impact on the development of the landscape. They did not want to recreate the past because the past was the past but to create a future biodiverse farmland that could become ecologically self-sustaining.

Dr Frans Vera had argued that before human impact, the behaviour of distant herbivores and their different grazing techniques which included disturbing the bark and breaking branches, digging up and rooting and trampling grasses, together with crapping everywhere with seeds and nutrients would have created a great mix of habitats suitable and more able to support a mix of relatives of the pig and cow.

Last week they took Jean Paul, Gerard and myself on a tour of the farm, all 200 acres (81 hectares) of it. It was remarkable what was already working as an experiment.

They had introduced free roaming cattle and pigs, a small goat herd. They had recently introduced ten European bison. These bison had been donated by an anonymous donor from Russia, who had heard of this experiment and wanted to support it.

The anonymous donor was of course Vladimir and Anna Petrova. Madeline and Giles Pertwee had kept them updated on what was happening in La Croix de Bois and this was too good an opportunity not to do something.

Interestingly, the local deer were taking advantage. They had not seen any evidence of wild boar but time would tell. The absence of any hunters as this was farmland encouraged these animals and of course the fact that the local hunt group was still suspended following the unfortunate accident of a known criminal from Nantes all those years ago.

And that was not all. The impact on wildlife has started to be stunning. It was remarkable how quickly this happened. Freed of the strangling presence of the building known as Guys' Cliff and its owners, it is almost as if everything from the earth to the trees to the wildlife had taken a huge breath of fresh air.

Already there are nightingales and doves, even more birds of prey who have ever greater quantities of mice and other small rodents to feed on.

We heard the woodpeckers and we saw the butterflies and moths and bees for ourselves. At night, the couple told us, they listened to the sound of owls and watched the bats in the twilight.

Guys' Cliff is no longer known as Guys' Cliff. The Mayor and the commune declared it *'La Place Verte' (the Green Place).* It has been reclaimed and embraced by nature and by La Croix de Bois. The French couple were only too happy to pass their smallholding on to manage this wonderful natural habitat. Between us we have named it the Sanctuary.

Chapter 29 - The Khalils

Much to Fardis' delight and to be honest, all of us, Yara was awarded a scholarship to study in Paris. She was also offered a placement at a fashion house there, as part of the course.

Jemal was playing regularly for the Dinan Lehon football team and was also helping out with the coaching of the girls football team at the club. He was also a year away from qualifying as an electrician.

Ibrahim was also one year away from completing his apprenticeship as an ebeniste and worked also with two local men on roofing and furniture repair.

Amira and Akira were happy at school and a feature of the village as they were always together. Farid was an immensely happy man to see them all doing so well and his thoughts were of the kindness of strangers in Jordan, the O'Keefes and people here in La Croix de Bois. Their kindness had helped him to find a better life for his children.

He stood looking at his 150 bee hives on La Place Verte, what used to be Guys' Cliff. Once Karen and Alain had been offered the chance to run the new experimental farm it had been a no-brainer to ask Farid to introduce the bees to the farm and he had been delighted. The hives that Ibrahim had built with him had been transported to the new farm and over time the hives were developing.

Farid found his favourite quiet spot under a twisted willow tree and sat down. This is where he spoke most days to Fatima, his dead wife and told her how much he missed her, how her children and her niece were doing and how different some of the techniques were for keeping bees in Brittany to the heat in Syria.

He told her how the honey tasted. He told her that it would be time to try and find their own house and how wonderful Ryan and Rose Marie O'Keefe had been to them.

When he finished speaking to Fatima, he kissed the trunk of the tree and told her how much he loved her and would speak with her tomorrow and he returned to his beloved bees.

Chapter 30 - The inspector moves to the village

Perhaps the most unexpected and remarkable thing that happened in the last two years was:

Inspector Didier Lauren moved into La Croix de Bois. He bought a small house on the edge of the village next to the house of Janine and Arthur Barnes – yes, the so-called Gestapo House.

He bought the house just as he was retiring. When he told me the news that he had bought the house I was surprised but delighted. When I asked him why he had moved to La Croix de Bois, he could not fully explain it properly.

'I know, I must be mad but there was this kind of pull to come and look at the house I now own. I was determined to wait to retire and then see how I felt about what to do and where to go. I have been an Inspector for many years and it has been my life.'

'I have to confess that it has been my addiction. I have been absorbed in being an Inspector and solving crimes and investigating incidents.'

'I was determined to wait and look over the horizon once

the dust had settled. This was sensible both intellectually and emotionally. So what did I do? I bought a house here in the middle of trying to finish work. Utter madness.'

'Utter madness' I had agreed.

'I cannot explain it. I have come to the one place where I never managed to solve a crime. That poor old man confessed to the bloody Mayor in the middle of my investigations on the murder of your friend Roger and the murderer was never on my radar.'

'Then, I never solved who was delivering the red monk money,' he said looking straight at me.'

Also, the shooting - all I knew was that it was not one of those hunters. That man, Henri Lascalle had no family to mourn him and seemingly no friends. Plenty of enemies but that is not the issue. He was murdered and my job was to find the murderer and I never did.'

The Inspector threw his hands into the air.

'Now' he continued, 'there is the mysterious disappearance of that man Castide. I think he was at Guys' Cliff when the plane hit it but I have no evidence. Everywhere else I solved crimes. Apart from one murder years ago in St

Pierre, I solved every case I ever had over twenty years. I had a great record but here.....nothing' he concluded.

I smiled at him and suggested 'perhaps the village has invited you here to live because it has things that it will need you to do?

'Do not jest my friend. This is a strange place, this place you call paradise. I hope I will fit in here.'

We had been sitting in his new garden, having a drink

'I have no doubt you will fit in here. Sante' I raised my glass to ex-inspector Didier Lauren.

'Sante' he replied.

I sat looking at the Inspector and remembered the murder of the man in St Pierre – he had been poisoned with hemlock and no-one knew why he had been murdered and no-one knew by whom.

Chapter 31 - Adieu.

I am sitting looking across the lake. There are ripples across the surface from the wind. Being near still water gives me a feeling of calm and serenity, which I have no doubt I share with most of us.

You are no doubt surprised that I am sitting by the lake and not at the bar being served a fine glass of wine by Marcel or Maria.

I am having one of those quiet reflective moments that sitting outdoors brings.

You are reminded, that you are part of nature and its cycles. Outdoors, I am faced with the recognition that I am nothing more than a tiny little bundle of atoms forged into a human being, of which there are now seven billion of us increasingly crowded on mother earth, no different from the birds and the bees.

La Croix de Bois is not crowded, even when all the tourists are here and everyone who has a second home here. It is not a busy city or a slum where millions are living cheek by jowl together. So I have time and space to think and of course reflect.

I have forgotten completely how long I have trodden this earth, because as you grow older, years seem to become meaningless and the seasons seem to come and go faster.

Perhaps it is convenient not to count the years.

The years and events also seem to merge together and it is hard to understand how suddenly names and incidents erupt in your head from the past from seemingly nowhere.

I know the years pass but my time in La Croix de Bois seems timeless.

I do not know whether there will be more tales to tell in such a small and insignificant place. But why Didier Lauren chose La Croix de Bois makes me wonder. Why Gerard and the Professor returned after their travels around the globe. How I came to be here. With them all here, I am sure that there will be things to tell.

We all have our individual reasons and answers but I do wonder whether it really is that simple.

Last week, the Mayor had invited Airman Thierry Lloris and his wing commander to come to a thank you reception at saving the village by managing to turn his plane away from the village before he had ejected from it.

Airman Thierry Lloris was very self-effacing. He explained very simply that he knew that he could not leave the plane because it was diving straight towards a village below. He knew that he would have to try to steer it away from La Croix de Bois. In that instant he accepted that basically he was going to die if the plane did not obliterate the village.

He said that he felt strangely calm and at the same time, a bizarre thing happened.

He said that afterwards, he thought that it was a gust of wind that moved the plane northwards as the controls that he was struggling with suddenly moved. It was as if time itself stood still and that he had heard others talk of such experiences and the plane moved to the north and as it did, then his chair was jettisoned out of the cockpit along with him.

He still found it hard to explain, even as he stood there in front of us. He would like to take the credit but it was something else that he could not explain.

When he said this, I felt a chill go up my spine to the back of my neck.

Thankfully, we have the beauty of not being able to peer into the future and know what's coming.

If that were the case for me, I would waste that talent by becoming rich from betting on horses and football matches and which politicians would get caught with his hand in the till or on someones wife or husband.

Until the next time - adieu

ABOUT LA CROIX DE BOIS AND ITS INHABITANTS

La Croix de Bois does not exist as a village. It represents a number of fine villages that you will see across Brittany. It has been located in the department of the Cotes d'Armor and as a consequence many of the place names around it actually exist as does the history and the folklore, the fables and the superstitions.

The Characters in the books are all 100% fictitious but you cannot move through life without meeting fabulous and bizarre people who leave their mark on you and their influences and stories cannot help but spill into the pages of anything that is being written.

It has been a privilege meeting so many people over the years and listening to their stories and adventures but for the purposes of these books, there are no friends or foes hidden in these characters, just influences and good thoughts as it should be.

Personally, I would like to live in La Croix de Bois, as it sounds a great place but I am equally lucky with where I do live and with the people around me

Andy Stonard

THANKYOU

Sandy who lives in the same village as me, read the first two books and pointed out in the nicest possible way, a number of typos and mistakes, which we had all missed previously.

Therefore, when he offered to edit this book, I welcomed him with open arms and now thank him because he was able to steer me with some of the plot as well as a lot of my grammer. I am extremely grateful.

Secondly to Garry, a good friend who diligently worked on the technical and design side of this book. Like many of us who know him, we would be lost without him – thank you.

To David Elliott from when I met him at Quartet books, who sadly passed away recently, who stuck by me with my draft of 'in search of the ancients' and supported me into making it a book, which gave me the encouragement to carry on writing.

To my many friends, acquaintances and neighbours past and present - it has been a delight moulding little parts of them all into the characters in La Croix de Bois. It has been a delight and a pleasure to have met and to get to know so many interesting, caring and fun people. They thankfully far far outnumber those who make life unpleasant with their greed and selfishness.

And of course to Teresa my wife, who in France was

officially a concubine until we were married in 2017. Jean Baptiste, (our friend, not the killer in the first book) kindly explained that men usually leave their wife for a concubine rather than marrying a concubine.

Printed by Amazon Italia Logistica S.r.l.
Torrazza Piemonte (TO), Italy